Corrupt Covenant

RORI BLEU

ROSIE CHAPEL

First printing: 2023
ISBN: 978-0-6459731-2-9 (eBook)
ISBN: 978-0-6459731-3-6 (Paperback)

Ulfire Pty. Ltd.
P.O. Box 1481
South Perth
WA 6951
Australia

Cover Design: R Norman
Cover Image: Canva/Deposit Photos
Designed in Canva
Internal images: Canva/Deposit Photos.
Created using appropriate licences.

Acknowledgments

RORI BLEU

Contrary to my usual form, there will be no fancy acknowledgments.

Simply, I want to thank Kirsten Miller for her love of all things dark and paranormal.

To my co-author, Rosie Chapel, for her love of history, being able to understand and fancy-up my writing, and demanding accuracy. Oh… and for humorously thinking she would never be conned into writing a book like this.

Acknowledgments

ROSIE CHAPEL

Thank you, Melanie, for your unwavering support and ability to bolster my confidence when it falters.

Thank you to my incredible family — for everything.

Once again, my co-author has dragged me kicking and screaming out of my comfort zone.

What started with a 'would you mind running your eyes over this?' ended up with me being wholly invested in this amazing novella… like that was in *any* way unexpected.

Thank you, Rori, for refusing to let me rest on my sadly maligned laurels.

Corrupt Covenant

Rori Bleu
Rosie Chapel

Prologue

Decebalus lay bleeding, his throat slit by his own hand. Although the fatal wound coaxed the veil of death to obscure his gaze, it was not swift enough. The Roman soldier approaching on horseback loomed larger with every passing second.

He knew the warrior carried orders from Emperor Trajan to collect him as a war prize for daring to attack the Roman provinces south of the Danube. Decebalus was not about to be paraded through Rome as a defeated king.

One final glance skywards to savour the dazzling blue, he closed his lids, awaiting his end.

Instead of the gentle murmur of the brook nearby ferrying him to the otherworld, a deep rumble reverberated around him; the sound becoming words.

"Human, are you such a coward, you would take your own life?"

"Death, cease your mockery of me," Decebalus's once stri-

1

dent intonation was wearied. "Do your job and whisk me away before the Romans advance any closer."

"Open your eyes and look at me," the voice commanded.

"I would rather not. Bad enough, I witnessed my allies flee and my men die from your pestilence even before we rallied for war." Decebalus countered. "To behold your hideous countenance is more than any man should be required to—"

"Silence, you impertinent creature," the voice bellowed.

A stomp accompanied the order. The ground beneath Decebalus quaked, the stream heaved momentarily, water overflowing its banks.

Cautiously opening one eye, Decebalus squinted at the Roman who appeared to be frozen in place. The man's mount balanced precariously on a single leg, mid-stride. It's billowing mane motionless.

The daylight, brilliant in its intensity moments ago, had dimmed.

"I am not Death. Quite the opposite, fool," the voice boomed. "I am here to offer you a chance to restore your life, your dignity, and your family."

Decebalus peered in the other direction. A colossal dark form blotted out the sun, and he realized, with no small amount of disbelief, who... or, in this case... *what* demanded his attention.

An infuriated black dragon.

Decebalus gawked, his other eye popped open.

The terror which suffused Decebalus at the sight of this apparition was greater than any imagined torture inflicted by Trajan or the Roman Legions.

His gaze locked with the dragon's piercing red eyes.

To his amazement, the hulking creature did not possess the rutted, leathery flesh of lore.

In fact, Decebalus considered his unexpected companion's appearance to be sleek and regal.

Mere inches apart, a sulfurous stench cured his nostrils when the dragon snorted at him.

"Vile creature, be gone. I pray for the underworld to claim me for my sin of pride."

"Leaving your wife and children to take your place on the Roman slave blocks? If that is your wish, you are more pitiful than I judged initially."

"It is not your place to judge me. As for my family, this is the only way I can ensure Trajan will not hunt them down. They are protected by—"

"The same treacherous curs who declared their loyalty to you? Even now they are casting lots as to who will be the one to deliver your family into your enemy's hands.

"Maybe stop wallowing in your guilt and failure, and listen to my offer. I promise you power and wealth beyond your wildest imagination."

"You speak with the tongue of the Great Deceiver. Assuredly, your pledge is as empty as my future."

"If your fate is so bleak, what have you to lose considering an alternative?"

"Fine, since you seem determined to delay my demise until I have listened to you, speak."

The dragon rose to face the lands stretching south to the mighty river and, his tone impassive, elaborated, "All I seek from you is to rid my land of these invaders."

Decebalus narrowed his eyes. "What do you think I have been trying to do? I have fought and bled for these lands, they belong to me."

The dragon huffed, "Which will be of little use to you in the afterlife.

"As for questioning the virtue of my intentions, you depended on those whose ulterior motives were far more devious. I, on the other hand, am desirous only of a free and peaceful land."

"You are a formidable demon. Would it not be easier to take matters into your own... errr... claws? The sight of you would send the legions scurrying back to Rome like vermin."

"There, my friend, lies the problem. I am but a myth to humans. Even you doubted me at first. I could destroy mankind if I sought to, but that is not my will, and to offer this arrangement to a less... honorable candidate, shall we say, would be misguided indeed. Not everyone can be trusted, as you have discovered.

"Doubtless, the same warriors would rise against me in search of their own sovereignty. Many of my kind have already succumbed to that fate. I do not plan to follow suit.

"Within you and your descendants, I perceive a unique determination and, dare I say, the same objective. A land purged of their relentless plunder."

Wordlessly, Decebalus contemplated the dragon, then, "Hitherto, I have failed to defeat the Romans, how is it possible for me to be triumphant now?"

"Because, until now, neither you nor your offspring possessed my power. With your allegiance, the invincibility of your heirs in any conflict is guaranteed. I will whisper victory in their ears. None shall conquer your blood."

"What becomes of our bargain if—"

"*If?*" the dragon interrupted contemptuously, a human word he detested.

"I mean... *once* we have succeeded?"

"As I vowed... eternal peace and prosperity for you and your people."

"How could I refuse such an auspicious agreement? Oh, I know, I am but moments from death and that rider, once you undo whatever magic you used to freeze time, will collect my head."

The dragon chuckled.

"Human, I enjoy your cynicism. Watch."

The dragon's chest swelled and he exhaled a torrent of fire which consumed Decebalus.

The king's throat burned for a moment. His hand flew to the wound, stunned to find it cauterized, and the blood from the gruesome gouge had vanished.

Rising, he discovered his heart pounding within his chest at a rate he had never felt before. His vitality and energy exceeding his recall.

"What of the warrior?" Decebalus asked, disconcerted to register he was alone.

In his mind, he heard the dragon reply, "Walk past him. I have left him the treasures he was sent to collect."

In the dust at his feet, Decebalus saw a charred head and right hand.

"Trajan will not believe this is me."

"He will because it is what he desires the most in his life. Your defeat has blinded him to the truth. Once he awakes from his delusion, it will be too late."

The king liked the sound of that plan, and did as he was told. As he passed the horse, he brushed his fingers along its flank as though to verify this entire experience was not a pre-death illusion.

Decebalus trudged back to his encampment, one last caveat from the dragon following on his heels. One which was passed down the generations.

"I swear protection in exchange for your fealty but, be warned, should any of your progeny dare break our accord, they will know nothing but eternal damnation."

Decebalus mumbled, "Is that not something you ought to have told me beforehand?"

"And miss savoring the taste of your human emotion of shock? Hardly."

The dragon's laughter pealed around Decebalus's head.

The one *minor* detail the dragon chose to withhold was that the king would never see the covenanted peace.

Every pact needs a sacrifice to seal the deal, the dragon justified.

It was another hundred and fifty years until the Romans withdrew from Dacia, bringing the pledge to fruition.

Chapter One

1106 AD

F rom the balcony of her fortress, Magdalina watched as the combined forces approached her gates. At the head of each, noble landowners who, on bended knee, had sworn their steadfast loyalty to her in hope of surviving the hordes from the East.

Their duplicity soured her gut.

Bribed by the very same enemy with avowals of wealth and prestige at her expense, they had turned their swords against her.

Magdalina glanced at the stained glass behind her. Proudly, it displayed the Dragoš coat of arms, her family's legendary claim to its power. The black dragon clutching a vivid white shield, stained with its blood in defense of her lineage.

The stories of how, a thousand years ago, the mighty beast had appeared from the depths of the nether regions to rescue her illustrious ancestor from the brink of death and the onslaught of a crazed mass intent on seizing his realm, still rang in her ears.

How this same creature aided subsequent rulers to repel threats from beyond their borders, of establishing a stable and prosperous peace.

In reality, history, like the legends it spawned, was little more than a tale which evolved and became embellished down the ages.

Magdalina knew no such savior existed, prepared to materialize from the stormy skies to save her land or heritage. "You are less effective than a child's bedtime fable," she spat at the image.

She could hear the wheels of the battering rams squealing as they rolled closer to the fortress, accompanied by the clamour of guttural voices and the clattering of swords pounding against shields.

Drawing her own blade, she smashed the stained glass into a shower of glittering pieces, commanding, "Return to your lair. You are of no use here."

The commotion from the armies at the gates, as well as the crash from the balcony propelled Magdalina's general to her side.

"My Queen, I need to spirit you away from here before it is too late."

"No, my dear Cristoff, we are well passed too late. If this night is to be the end of my bloodline, so be it. Come, my friend and escort me into eternity."

Cristoff dropped to one knee, cupping his queen's smaller hand in his. He placed one last kiss on her onyx ring. "It will be my pleasure, Magdalina."

Hearing her name on his lips brought a smile to hers. As

children, they had played and learned and laughed together, using their given names freely, not to mention other, less… polite monikers.

After Magdalina acceded to the throne, he had not presumed to speak it so casually. He was born to serve her, to give his life for her if necessary. Formality became ingrained; she deserved that respect.

Now, they were equals once again, each determined to wreak vengeance on the traitors resolved to usurp her reign.

Magdalina stood on the balcony to hail her devoted troops gathered in the courtyard below, "To battle. Glory and a warrior's grave awaits us all. We fight to the last."

A roar went up from the crowd, reaching a crescendo as Cristoff and she descended the stairs to take the lead.

"Let them know death, my friends," were the last words any heard from Magdalina as she plowed headlong into the throng of enemy soldiers.

The clash of steel on steel ricocheted off the curtain of the Carpathian mountains, soaring in craggy grandeur beyond the stronghold, to float back in discordant echoes.

By sunrise, the castle lay in smoldering ruins. The bodies of the fallen from both sides consumed in its flames.

As for the two who led the charge against the greedy nobles, in defense of Magdalina's right to rule, theirs was not an honorable demise.

Magdalina, who had bested her general in the number put to the sword, glanced over her shoulder curious to see whether he had equaled her count.

In horror, she witnessed Cristoff being cut down by a cowardly slash from behind. She abandoned the fray and fell to her knees beside him, weeping as he died in her arms.

Posthumously pronounced a servant of evil, Cristoff's body was dragged around the walls of the fortress before being impaled on a pike at the gate.

His head, arms, and legs were severed from the torso and stuffed into the saddle bags of three separate horses, who were swatted with a thorny branch, sending them racing in different directions.

Cristoff's punishment was merciful compared with Magdalina's. Captured alive, she was stripped naked, shackled with a length of thick rope normally used to moor ships, and paraded past the surviving enemy soldiers to the banks of the Danube.

Their crude attempts to humiliate and degrade her, failed when she refused to give them the satisfaction of pleading for clemency.

Lashed to a tree, Magdalina's arms were stretched above her head, and her hands nailed to the trunk in a makeshift crucifixion, from where she watched the men who had bayed for her death, cobble together a huge raft, while others rowed across the mighty Danube.

Determined to see the defeated queen banished from her lands forever, a small section of the river was re-routed, temporarily, while a deep pit was dug into the bank and lined with boulders.

Once complete, the raft, loaded with a lead sarcophagus was hauled to the opposite side, where it was buried in the pre-made grave.

Although it was too far for Magdalina to behold the result of their exertions, she knew it did not bode well.

The second day arrived to find her clinging to life, streaks of drying blood from her wounds marring her body in dark rivulets. Cut down from the tree, she was trussed up in the same rope which had led her like cattle to the slaughter, and lowered into a plain wooden casket.

Before they closed the lid, the patriarch of the local

Orthodox eparchy stood over Magdalina, clutching a cross. Scowling at her, he decreed, "In the name of the most Holy, I proclaim you a festering seed of Satan.

"The fact you survived the righteous punishment of our Lord, and refused to beg for the mercy which would allow you to pass over, exacerbates your guilt."

A young nobleman, fearing Magdalina would return to exact her revenge, implored, "Please, Father Mikael, part her lips, I beseech you."

The patriarch stepped back and nodded at two of the guards who wrenched Magdalina's jaw open. A gurgled howl rolled from her throat.

The young man approached, holding a wooden spike carved from a crucifix. Signing the cross with it, he shoved it between Magdalina's lips, not stopping until it pierced the back of her mouth.

Magdalina flinched, not at the pain — although that was excruciating — but at the metallic taste of her blood oozing down her throat. Her eyes widened as the flow increased.

Focusing on the young man, she saw his other hand swing a rock downward. The blow drove the stake through her spine and into the casket's base, pinning her in place.

Magdalina's scream was garbled by the shaft of wood.

Leaving her to drown in her own blood was perverse enough, the fact these men perpetrated their atrocities in the name of the Lord, proved their *religion* was nothing more than a charade to justify their crimes.

A shadow obscured the light, she felt the length of hemp shift fractionally, and the tip of something cold and sharp was raked down her body; her skin pebbled.

"Something to… aid you into Hell, should Lucifer prove tardy in recouping his servants…" the object was tucked into the bonds circling her calf, "… but not immediately." the speaker mocked.

Their final act of spite, tossing Cristoff's heart in with her. The bloodied organ bounced off her hip to land a hair's breadth from her fingers.

As the lid was sealed in place, she heard another of the noble's mock, "Appreciate our gift, *your majesty*. You are interned in perpetuity with your snivelling lackey, but the Lord will never allow you to reach him."

Spine-chilling dread consumed Magdalina when the casket was elevated. It did not take a great intellect to suppose they were relaying her across the river to where they had secreted the lead sarcophagus.

The splash of water accompanied by an undulation motion confirmed her suspicions.

Not being able to see her destination or trust her *escorts*, magnified Magdalina's nightmare but, soon, the rocking was replaced by a sinking sensation, and the scrape of metal on metal.

In the blackness of the coffin, she listened to the noise of something heavy being piled on top of the lid.

Gradually, this was superseded by another, more restful, sound.

Starting from the base of the sarcophagus Magdalina heard water lapping at the sides, filling the space around her.

Her enemies had removed the diversion, releasing the Danube to flow again. Its currents became her perpetual lullaby, delivering Magdalina into a hazy slumber.

Death refused to grant her complete respite.

Throughout the millennium which followed, Magdalina was disturbed time and again by strange rumblings. The din, louder and closer than any thunderstorm.

She speculated that the descendants of those who had condemned her here, had advanced their ability to murder one another.

With each deafening crash from above, Magdalina screamed for them to cease the folly being committed.

It was a waste of effort. Her voice could not breach the wood, lead, stone, and water entombing her, but it made her feel better.

Drifting off, she concentrated on the comforting melody of the Danube singing in rhythm with the beating of Cristoff's heart. Despite being unable to reach it, knowing it was near, meant she had not lost him.

While the remnants of her sanity tried to convince her it was her own heart she could hear, her emotions held firm in the belief Cristoff still lived... in some form... somewhere out there waiting for her to find him.

There was one welcome, if *anything* about her confinement could be described as welcome, development. The rope by which they had constrained her, loosened and, eventually, yielded its hold completely.

Not that she could take advantage of this emancipation, but her sense of claustrophobia eased marginally.

The weapon — for what else could it be? — her captors had tucked into the bindings, remained beyond her grasp, and she had long abandoned any hope of using the implement to end her life.

Whenever the din from above receded, Magdalina sank into her deathless sleep, resigned to the fact this was her doom... until the river gauged it time for the sins of the past to be revealed and atoned for.

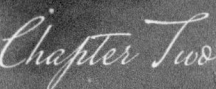

Chapter Two

Romania
October 1990

O ver time, the frequency of intrusions to Magdalina's slumber, escalated and, what began as an occasional uproar above her, raged for longer intervals.

She had also noticed the customary chill of the river being supplanted by, in almost indistinguishable degrees, an appreciable warmth.

It was traumatic enough to be suspended between life and death. The increased heat inside the lead sarcophagus made purgatory sound like a delightful stroll around the fortress gardens.

Magdalina also divined the pressure and depth of the water appeared to be diminishing; until one day, the Danube was rippling around only the base of the tomb.

Has someone dammed the river again, this time to free me? she ruminated. *Surely, none alive remember me.*

Through the ancient casing, she heard people shouting in languages, she did not understand, and was unable to prevent a spasm of trepidation at the clunk of stones being dislodged from their placement on the lid.

Maybe Death's angels have come for me.

The annoying racket of rock scraping against the metal subsided.

Unexpectedly, the casket teetered as Magdalina registered she was being hoisted. Almost immediately, the upward motion stopped, followed by the impression of being rotated.

Someone yelled, "Do not drop it. Goddammit, get that truck down here."

The repetitive squelch of something heavy being pushed over mud and gravel ceased, and her tomb was dropped with more haste than care, onto a hard surface.

Although the commotion made no sense to Magdalina, she did work out that it related to whatever she had been placed onto.

The *thunk* provoked a flurry of angry words, presumably from the person in charge of operations.

"Jesus Christ. Can't you lot do anything right? We have no idea how old this thing is or the condition of anything which might be inside." The tone moderated. "Please, I would be tremendously grateful if you could get this to the Institute without causing any more damage."

Opening her eyes, Magdalina spied the slenderest sliver of light illuminating her space. For the briefest moment, she saw something she had not seen since this nightmare began… blue sky.

It did not last. Something was flung over the lid, obliterating her cherished view. The peculiar sounds reminiscent of rope stretching suggested the sarcophagus had been secured to what Magdalina imagined was a large wagon.

Instead of the crack of a whip and whinnying of horses, she heard a growl similar to that of the war creatures she had grown accustomed to over the ages.

A sharp jerk then a gentle swaying indicated they had started moving, and Magdalina pondered whether her unknown destination was Hell.

Dating back to 1834, the Vasile Pârvan Institute of Archaeology was the oldest research facility of its kind in Romania, specializing in the history and archaeology of the prehistoric, ancient, and medieval periods.

Its reputation for excellence had attracted international experts since its inception, all eager to participate in one of the many excavations or study programs.

It was also Magdalina's destination.

As the truck slowed to a stop, it bumped the edge of the loading dock at the rear of the Institute's laboratories, jolting Magdalina's casket violently. A rude awakening after an eternity languishing in relatively undisturbed darkness.

Oh, to be queen again, so I might remonstrate with these workers regarding their negligence.

She listened to the men complain about something, still unable to understand.

Magdalina felt the coffin move again. The grating noise beneath her caused her to grind her teeth against the wooden stake still lodged in her mouth.

Wanting to cry out, to implore them to cease the incessant noise, she was startled and relieved when her wish was granted, as the casket appeared to float upwards. The sedate rocking lulled Magdalina into slumber... until whatever conveyed her, came to a halt.

Curses were hurled at the clumsy dolts who had mishandled her box and any family members who might have the ability to procreate.

A cacophony of voices and footsteps surrounded her. Listening intently, Magdalina realized she was, inexplicably, gaining comprehension.

She concluded the screams and commands issued during the countless wars waged atop her resting place had contributed to her accidental education.

"I tell you, the box should not be opened until we have had more time to examine it," Magdalina heard the voice of an elderly man argue. "You and your colleagues in America may be haphazard in your techniques, but here in Romania—"

Romania? Magdalina mused. *Did the Romans return to oust the Magyars and regain the lands they vacated willingly? Why would the nobility allow them to occupy my kingdom after so many centuries?* Questions to which she had no answers... yet... or maybe ever.

"Doctor Enache, rest assured, we shall exercise extreme diligence when removing the contents."

How impertinent, reducing me to an inanimate object, Magdalina fumed.

"Do not be naive, Williamson," the older voice, presumably the aforementioned Dr. Enache, ranted angrily. "Yes, while the handling is my responsibility, it is the contents which are of greater concern. Someone took extraordinary measures to ensure this box was never found, nor whatever is interred therein be able to escape."

The one called Williamson scoffed, "Surely, sir, a man of science such as yourself, is not a captive of local superstitions and folklore.

"Anything in this sarcophagus has long since lost its ability to harm you in any way… well, maybe with the exception of an ancient bacteria waiting to attack you. I cannot imagine it contains anything more lethal than a family's cache, or moldy papers or, and more likely, a pile of bones."

"Doubt me all you want, Williamson, but stories have been passed down my bloodline—"

"Just as I said, Enache, stories. Now, get your men to help me remove this lid."

The scratching generated by whatever the men were doing on the other side of the chest made Magdalina wince.

The abrupt silence informed her, the upper lead lid had been breached. A rush of cool air filled the inner coffin. Magdalina struggled not to cough when it hit her.

Unadulterated joy at the prospect of being liberated from the abominable box engulfed her. She prayed the first thing those opening the casket did was remove the wooden stake from her mouth, so she could enunciate her gratitude.

"Gentlemen, lift the wooden lid, carefully," Williamson instructed. "On three."

Magdalina heard the wood splinter, and bright light flooded her coffin. No matter how hard she tried to blink it away, its intensity seemed to grow in severity, with no relief to be had. She attempted to shield her eyes, but was unable to move.

To her dismay, she discovered why.

In the reflection of a large, silvered dome above her, Magdalina saw what remained of her once renowned beauty. To say time had been kind to her would have been a cruel joke.

The shriveled visage leering back at her was grotesque. Pallid flesh, dried and stretched taut from eons of hovering on the brink of death, prevented her from closing her lids.

The muscles along her arms had atrophied and withered away.

In place of shimmering azure eyes, black spectral orbs filled her sunken sockets.

Her once glossy, raven hair, painfully coiffured by her maid servants, had faded to a lusterless ash white.

Repulsed, Magdalina wanted to scream at the hideous creature into which she had deteriorated. Even had she possessed the vocal cords to utter a sound, the accursed spike wedging her jaws apart hindered any such attempt.

After a few moments of abject terror, something in the dome caught Magdalina's curiosity.

Her canine teeth had become elongated and more defined.

How is that possible? Did the wood actually sharpen my teeth?

"Dear God," Magdalina heard the older man exclaim in what sounded like her language. "I said your recklessness would be the death of us, Williamson."

Williamson, she was beginning to recognize his voice, replied in the same tongue, "My good doctor, this poor creature has long since passed the point of harming anyone."

"You impetuous fool, can you not see she is an ancient vampiress? Look, traces of rope, hemp probably, encircle the body, those who buried her went to great lengths to restrain her."

"Come now, are you telling me, you believe that, if I remove this stake…"

Williamson yanked the rotting wood from Magdalina's mouth, the room echoed with gasps and shrieks as the spectators braced themselves for the worst.

"…she can do anything other than continue her rapid decomposition, unless we get her into the cooler?"

"Williamson, as God's servants, we would serve humanity better by destroying her."

The American sighed his exasperation. "Enache, she has not leapt from her casket to bite your throat. If you insist on clinging to your archaic doctrine, I shall have no alternative but to ask you to leave."

"With pleasure, Doctor Williamson, and may God have mercy on your soul for disturbing this monster's internment."

Magdalina — wishing she knew what was meant by a vampiress, and what threat they posed — heard the rustle of hurried footsteps, as Enache, presumably, fled.

Out of Magdalina's line of sight, Williamson pointed to one of the men who had helped bring in the sarcophagus. "Slide your arms under her legs and, very carefully, help me maneuver her onto the gurney."

She remained unaware the man, confounded by what he had seen in the coffin, shook his head, but she did hear another pair of feet scurrying away, then several more as the rest of Dr. Enache's assistants followed on his heels, like rats from a sinking ship, leaving Williamson alone.

"You backwoods bastards," he excoriated. "We live in the twentieth century, myth cannot hurt you."

He grumbled balefully about gullible fools, keenly aware, if he was going to salvage the remains, he would have to move them on his own.

He eased his arms under the corpse, disintegrating ropes and all, and lifted it cautiously, registering the body was not as cold as he expected. He chalked this up to the heat wave sweeping the whole of Europe or, and more feasibly, global warming.

Transferring the cadaver to the waiting gurney, he stifled an expletive when the head lolled. The accompanying snap sent shockwaves through him, fearing the skull was about to detach from the spine.

He placed the body on the clean sheet, with more

celerity than was his practice — brittle strands of hemp, slithering onto the pristine white cloth — and, meticulously, inspected the neck and throat for damage, relieved to find both intact.

This close examination led to another oddity.

Bearing in mind the conditions of internment, there should be no smell from remains of this age, yet a distinctive odor teased his nostrils. One normally associated with recent death when the flow of blood has yet to slow.

An anomaly necessitating further investigation.

Checking the coffin for anything he might have missed, Williamson noticed a lump of something where the woman's right knee had lain, and the glint of an object closer to the foot of the casket.

He grabbed a flashlight from the table next to him, clicked it on and swung the beam around the interior.

The glint turned out to be a short sword, reminiscent of a Roman *pugio*, with an intricately carved hilt. Despite its years under a decaying cadaver, it looked pristine, the blade still honed.

Gingerly Williamson lifted it out, hefting its weight in his gloved palm. A grim smile twisted his mouth as he put the item aside.

He pointed the torch at the mass, which, to his surprise, appeared to be a dehydrated organ.

As he reached in to recover the mysterious object, he caught his thumb against a jagged piece on the rim of the lead sarcophagus, tearing the examination glove and his flesh beneath it.

"Dammit. Can anything else go wrong?"

Before he could staunch the blood, a few beads dripped onto the desiccated relic, soaking into it and causing it, impossibly, to expand ever-so slightly.

"Great, one of the most significant archaeological finds in

Europe in God knows how long, and I'm contaminating it with the ineptitude of a first year college student.

Putting the artifact into a metal bowl, Williamson noted it resembled a heart...

How it has lasted this long, I have no idea.

Unable to answer his own question... right at that moment, he put the bowl between the woman's legs, and pushed the gurney into the waiting cooler.

He closed the heavy door, and joked, "It's getting late, dear lady. Please don't prove that silly old man right and try running away tonight."

Chapter Three

Oddly, the frigid darkness enveloping Magdalina once again was comforting. No doubt evoked from her existence in the cold depths of the Danube.

Interestingly, the chill was not wholly encompassing.

The metal bowl, shoved between her knees by the infuriating peasant, began to radiate a gentle heat which seemed to penetrate her dried flesh. More than that, Magdalina felt as though her leg muscles were being rejuvenated.

Concentrating on her hands, she willed her fingers to flex.

Pain… *pain?*… flared up her right arm as her index finger twitched. Gradually, panting through the glorious torture, Magdalina clenched each finger of her right hand until she had formed a fist, her nails digging into her palm.

While manipulating the now functioning hand, she attempted to repeat the exercise with her left arm, but it remained frozen in place.

That her dominant left side — the side from which retribution at the end of her sword was meted out — lay useless… no torment, no motion… kindled a trickle of panic.

Swallowing her alarm, Magdalina focused on her legs.

Pushing her left foot out, she wanted to make sure her entire left side had not been rendered immobile.

The warmth had spread from her knee to the ball of her foot, and her toes tingled with the pricks of a thousand needles. The same phenomenon was occurring in her other foot.

Magdalina tried to sit up, only to bang her head on the lid of the metal box.

As she fell backwards, she heard a soft throb. Initially, she thought it was her ears playing tricks on her; simply the vibration of a long empty cranium connecting with an unforgiving surface.

The throb did not abate.

Composing herself, Magdalina concentrated on the source of the thready beat. A sound she associated with her confinement.

The longer she listened, the steadier it became. Stretching her arm, her hand landed on the cool brim of the bowl wedged between her thighs.

Tentatively, she dipped one finger into its depths, touching something sticky. Her nail scraped across a fibrous shape; a coppery tang teased her nostrils.

A pang hit her stomach, and she was assailed by a hunger unlike anything she had experienced.

Scouring the bowl, Magdalina lifted her hand to her parched lips and lapped greedily. Her tongue slithered between her fingers to catch any stray droplets. The more she supped, the more pronounced the thrumming.

The erratic beating, and the life-giving blood, which Magdalina could not stop guzzling, could only come from the mass in the bowl — the remnants of Cristoff's heart.

Magdalina marveled as it pulsed in her grasp. Images of

curling against his chest, as they lay in her chambers, secretly sharing her bed, reared up in her mind.

With them, an unfamiliar voice, fueling the loss of her humanity, exhorted, "Do it girl. Drink from the very heart of your lover."

It was as though the unseen entity was performing an unholy mass.

"See how much protection *he* can provide you."

Unable to control herself, she brought it to her mouth, as her left hand burst from its slumber, scrabbling to intercede.

The struggle was for naught.

A loud bellow caused Magdalina's surroundings to quake and she questioned why no one else seemed to have heard.

"Do as I command. Sink your teeth into it and slake your thirst. Only then will you fulfill your debt to me."

"D-debt?" she whispered.

"Aye, girl. Your rejection of my gift to you and your line. You lost faith in me, and there is a price to pay."

Rapaciously, Magdalina plunged her fangs into Cristoff's heart. Its iron-rich flavor exploded in her mouth, and she savored the piquancy of his essence before gulping it down.

Curiously, the flow did not diminish. With each quaff, Magdalina was aware of her body being restored, until the last swallow triggered her long-dormant heart.

Subsumed by the feasting frenzy, the final few drops hit her tongue. They were the sweetest of all, leaving her aching for more.

"That's it, child. Burn the memory of your first taste into your brain and, with it, know you will remain in servitude to me until the days of this world cease."

"*No*," Magdalina screamed. "Never will I serve evil such as you."

"*Evil?*" The voice chuckled. "My dear, *dear* queen, evil

spelled backwards is live? Who bestowed on you the right to designate how I live as evil? Your ancestor chose to overlook it to his advantage."

"It is evil to tie me to a pledge made a millennium before my birth."

"Yet you partook of the fruits of that bargain."

"That was for the benefit of my subjects. I had no choice—"

"Until you decided I was no longer needed." A sigh whooshed through Magdalina's head. "You must face the consequences of your betrayal. Then and only then might you earn absolution."

"Betrayal," Magdalina scoffed. "Have you forgotten the hordes who betrayed—"

"Silence, fool. Someone is coming."

The voice left her brain.

Confused as to what drove it away, Magdalina strained to hear anything outside the metal box. She froze when she caught the gravelly tones of the older man who had cautioned Williamson about vampires.

Doctor Enache.

"If Williamson refuses to heed my warning, I will destroy this beast myself. May the good Lord forgive me for desecrating the body of this foul creature."

With a click, the mechanism imprisoning her was released. Light steamed into the box as the door swung open, and the tray on which her body rested, yanked out.

Expecting the light to dazzle her, Magdalina narrowed her eyes at the old man glaring down at her, holding aloft a wooden stake, poised to drive it into her heart.

Dr. Enache was flabbergasted to see, in place of a mummified corpse, a beguilingly naked female, who appeared equally astonished.

It took a moment for Enache to gather his wits.

Seizing the opportunity, Magdalina levered herself off the tray to tackle the doctor. Her limbs wound around him, her unnatural strength expelling the air from his lungs.

Struggling to break free of her grip, Enache attempted to slam her against the bank of refrigerator doors. Instead, the collision knocked the stake out of his hand, and it skittered across the tiled floor.

Detecting the woman's feverish panting against the side of his throat, Enache petitioned, "Please, Lord, show me mercy and rid the world of her."

Magdalina had other ideas.

Her breath caressed his ear. "Your god has deserted you, old man. You belong to me now."

Magdalina could not believe the words slipping from her lips, nor the demonic tone which delivered them.

Rearing back like a cobra, she struck, piercing Enache's jugular. She did not know how she located it while the man thrashed frantically, but the burst of blood coating her fangs and pouring into her mouth made any other consideration a waste of thought.

This man's blood lacked the robust vitality of Cristoff's. The inferior taste might be disappointing, but she was not about to squander it. Magdalina held out hope, the last mouthful would be as gratifying as her lover's.

Enache's knees buckled with each gulp, and Magdalina sank with him onto the floor, refusing to relinquish her hold or her exsanguination of the dying archaeologist.

The final trickle seeped down her throat, leaving Magdalina as disappointed as with the first drop.

Shuffling away from the drained corpse, Magdalina dragged her hand across her mouth, cringing when her fangs caught her own flesh.

In morbid curiosity, she watched the beads of blood gather at the scratches. Tilting her head, she dabbed her tongue on each. To her amazement, it tasted like Cristoff... but, immediately, caused her to retch.

Bitter, acidic liquid spewed over her lips, spraying Enache's body, which began to dissolve with a dreadful hiss.

The stench of death overwhelmed Magdalina, and oblivion claimed her.

The room was quiet when Magdalina opened her eyes. She could not comprehend how long she had been insensible. A glance at a row of windows in the upper part of the wall indicated it was still night.

Scrambling upright, she ran one hand over her body, discovering she was coated in a curdled slime from her breasts to her legs.

Upon further investigation, as she attempted to find her victim, Magdalina was horrified to register that she was covered with the residue of her first kill.

At her feet, a pool of black liquid, mixed with bone and clumps of dirt.

Her stomach threatened to empty again.

Magdalina swallowed the bile, realizing she had to hide the evidence. It would not be long before that Doctor Williamson returned to examine his latest discovery.

"Better you than me, old man."

Scooping up handfuls of Enache, Magdalina dumped the sludge onto the tray originally assigned to her.

After what felt like hours, she could get no more off the floor.

Desperate to finish the job, Magdalina used the white sheet, which had covered her in the cold box, to clean the floor, as well as herself. Neither was pristine, but might just pass muster if the inspection was cursory.

Finished, Magdalina was unsure how to dispose of the sheet, until she looked at the wall of silvery doors. One stood open; the one in which she had been confined.

It was a perplexing construction. The interior of her box was very cold, but the room maintained a comfortable temperature, prompting her to speculate as to its fabrication.

A clever way to keep food fresh, wholly unaware of the irony of that thought.

She tugged at the chunky handle of the adjacent box. The heavy door swung open soundlessly, and she thrust the sheet inside.

"That takes care of one problem…" she reviewed her state of undress, "…but I have another."

Surveying the room, Magdalina spotted a wooden post with stubby hooks, like antlers, sticking out of the top. On it hung several white, shapeless garments. Heedless of their purpose, she snagged one and slipped it on, wrestling with the peculiar fastenings, before foraging for suitable footwear.

Finding nothing, she spotted a pile of odd and very flimsy-looking looking slippers which might suffice until she could acquire something more practical.

Pulling them on, Magdalina went in search of a way out of the building. Opening the door, she noticed two slim plates affixed to the outside, one above the other

One was vaguely identifiable; the other, not dissimilar.

She read them out loud so as not to forget.

"Morgă," and the one underneath, "Morgue," which she pronounced phonetically, so it sounded something like morgyooee.

The words were reminiscent of the Latin, mortuārium.
The place of the dead.

Magdalina smiled grimly. "So the good Doctor Enache is among friends."

Chapter Four

Concerned she might run into someone and be captured, Magdalina tried to make herself inconspicuous.

She had already killed someone, even though the old man's demise was self-defense — bearing in mind he was about to impale her with that infernal stake — doing so meant it was essential to conceal her presence.

Perhaps the man, Williamson, would assume Enache had implemented his threat; the sludge on the metal slab, all that remained of the corpse in the sarcophagus. He might be vexed, but would he investigate further? She had no idea.

She surmised this same man had no interest in tracking down Enache to interrogate him on the matter, at least, not for the foreseeable future.

Magdalina was only partly grateful for the increasingly irritating slippers. They muffled her steps but, whenever she stopped, she skidded across the polished floor.

Spying a door at the end of the corridor, she risked everything by darting toward it.

Halfway there, a stray scent teased her nostrils, bringing her to a tumbling halt.

Howling in pain… this time *not* appreciating the stimulation… she cursed the improvised footwear.

Magdalina pulled herself upright and leaned against the wall to tug them off.

She groused under her breath, "If my exploits thus far were not loud enough to summon the palace guards, I daresay 'tis safe to walk barefoot."

Scrunching the slippers in her hand, she hurled them with all her might, their aimless glide downward in no way alleviating her aggravation.

Instead of grappling with the offending and unorthodox slippers, Magdalina concentrated her attention on the source of the aroma.

As with the heart, it was one with which she was acutely familiar.

Cristoff, where are you, my love? Where are they holding you captive? Please, dear Lord, please tell me his soul was not cursed like mine.

Despite the light from the bizarre torches, somehow enclosed within glass-like covers, burning brightly above her — the rooms behind the windows, placed at equidistant intervals along the gallery, were unlit, save one.

Closing her eyes, she allowed her heightened olfactory senses to guide her to where he was surely imprisoned. It seemed to be coming from where the dull glow spilled into the corridor.

Trusting her intuition, her steps led her to a door. Peering through the spotless pane of glass — a remarkable, not to mention useful, feature — Magdalina made out a large room, at the center of which stood a solid-looking table with a chair tucked underneath.

Illuminated by another of those clever torches, the dulled

surface was scattered with papers, papyrus scrolls, and manuscripts.

She pushed the door, but it refused to open. Scanning the wood paneling, she spotted the knob. Frowning, she jiggled it, then turned it with some vigor, gawking when it broke off in her hand, the other half of the knob dropping to the floor inside the room with a clatter.

Squinting through the resulting cavity, Magdalina spied a bar with a smaller hole. She attempted to manipulate it with her finger, but failed.

Disappointed, she checked the pockets of the costume she had borrowed. In one, her fingers brushed against something sturdy.

She withdrew the shiny, curved, metal tool. Its odd shape and size suggested it was a woman's knife, until it fell open as she examined it.

The tool turned out to be a miniature pair of shears. She had never seen a set so slender, or sharp... the latter revealed when she cut herself testing the edge.

Out of habit, she was about to suck the injured finger, quickly recalling what occurred the last time her own blood touched her lips. Judiciously, she wiped her maligned digit on the white coat.

"This must be a frock of a handmaid," Magdalene muttered out loud. "No male would have use for such a small implement."

That said, she believed it would be sufficient to move the bar holding the door closed.

Inching the shears into the hole, she grasped the bar between the tiny blades, wiggling the tool until she heard a *click*, and the door opened slowly.

To disguise her forced entry, Magdalena replaced the broken knob in the hole and pulled the door shut.

Inside the room, Magdalina breathed deeply. Cristoff's scent was so intoxicating, she felt giddy.

Reeling like a drunkard, and unsure how long she would remain cogent under the pall of the heady fragrance, she hurried to the table to comb through the stacks of documents.

Her position as royalty, necessitated that Magdalina become proficient in the various local dialects, and the written word of her people. Her tutor taken his role seriously, also ensuring his pupil was accomplished in Greek and Latin, and understood the administrative complexities of a bustling court.

Although she did not have to deal with invading Romans, as had some of her ancestors, she was compelled to contend with an all-powerful church in Rome determined to spread their faith to her lands.

This meant she found herself more deeply engrossed in the writings than was prudent.

She could not help herself.

The beautiful penmanship of the old texts was infinitely more pleasing to read than the bland print in the new. The calligraphy decorating the handwritten scrolls possessed a flourish lost through the generations.

While the documents came from different origins, from the corners of what was once Magdalina's realm to countries well beyond her borders, as far as she could discern, they shared a common thread. All appeared to be first-hand testimonies relating to the existence of assorted evil creatures dating back long before the birth of Christ.

More than a few contained the legend of the last ruler of the Dragoš dynasty and her missing tomb.

Curiously, none bore any mention of her name, nor her final resting place.

Along the margins, handwritten notes, some faded with

age, some she could not understand. Interestingly, they all looked to be authored by the same person.

Magdalina marveled at an intricately drawn dragon, complete with flames spurting from its mouth.

Scrawled next to the image, in her own language were the words, *What have you done with her?*

Even with the passage of time, Magdalina recognized the hand; one more adept at dueling than composing verse.

Echoes of the past swamped her. Two children determined to best each other at their lessons. A thin-faced tutor trying, desperately, to instill knowledge into the flighty pair, who were more interested in playing than reading. A tall, gangling youth, hoping to impress a maiden with his horsemanship.

Cristoff.

One of father's hogs could out-write you.

A wry smile teasing at her mouth, she picked up a flat object made of a thin material, which flexed in her grasp. Turning it over, she noticed it was the same on both sides, but something was pressed in between.

Prying apart the sides, her eyes widened at the interior. It contained sheets of the finest parchment she had ever seen. Her fingers were visible through a single page, which was gossamer smooth to her touch and, despite an apparently fragile construction, did not tear.

A new form of manuscript, made of silk perchance? she marveled, in awe of the scribe's skill. The binding felt durable, and so light.

Magdalina's smile morphed into a quiet chuckle, recollecting the times she had lugged weighty tomes at the behest of her tutor. She wagered, she could carry ten, nay twenty of these dainty books compared with one of her father's bound volumes.

Entranced, she turned the pages, identifying the same

handwriting as was in the margins of the manuscripts. Words filled each sheet, but were difficult to read because of the tightly packed lines.

She was about to sit down, intent on a more detailed perusal when the heavy tread of boots traversing the corridor interrupted.

Ducking behind the table, she prayed to the mythical 'good thief', crucified at the right hand of Jesus, to protect her crime from being uncovered.

The boots stopped near the door. Magdalina held her breath, well aware that, if anyone touched the knob, it would come off in their hand.

She saw a light flash through the little square of glass. The beam ranged across the space, landing on sundry furnishings.

The time it took the guard to examine the room was agonizing.

Magdalina knew she was in no danger of being appre-hended. The ease with which she had disposed of the one named Enache reassurance enough, but she did not want to repeat *that* graphic scene.

There are only so many places to secrete sloppy remains. Her lip curled sardonically.

The light veered away and the thud of the boots faded.

If she was to learn of Cristoff's whereabouts, Magdalina needed to find somewhere to hide in this dungeon.

She snatched the curious binding containing Cristoff's notes. "No sense leaving empty handed. I should like to read history's opinion of me."

Not quite steady on her feet, after eons without moving, Magdalina bumped into the table. A single sheet, from the ream of loosely organized documents, fluttered to the floor, along with a rectangular-shaped object which clattered loudly in the hush.

Unwilling to leave any trace of her intrusion, Magdalina stooped to retrieve them.

Scanning the paper, she saw it was hand scribbled missive in a language similar to her own. Some of the words were obscure, but Magdalina was able to comprehend the context.

Dr. Williamson,

Your new assistant, Sabina Radu, from the Budapest University will arrive early Sunday morning in readiness for the autopsy.

Her identity keycard has been included herewith, negating further delay.

I understand your preference to interview Miss Radu, prior to her being granted approval to join your team, but the timing of your discovery supersedes the usual protocols, and she comes highly recommended.

Sincerely,

Dr. Lupu

The note prompted Magdalina to think twice about stealing something as obvious as the good doctor's research notes.

"It will be the first thing he will look for once aware someone has been here uninvited," Magdalina convinced herself in undertones.

She studied the rectangular item.

It was hard and, on one side, a silvery strip. On the other, an etching... far more detailed than the icons from those in the chapel adjacent to the fortress... of a woman.

Magdalina squinted to read the wording under the image — Sabina Radu.

A wicked smile lit her face. "I ought to meet this Radu woman."

Chapter Five

Sunday Morning
7:00 AM

While the idea of working for the prestigious Dr. Christopher Williamson was something Sabina Radu could not pass up, giving up her only sleep-in of the week was another matter.

Worse, she had spent the last twenty minutes in the security office trying to get her clearance card, essential to access the labs. It took a call to the crotchety Dr. Lupu to verify her identity.

"Why is it my fault Doctor Williamson forgot to give you my ID?" she grumbled to the guard as he issued her a limited-use card.

The security guard's reply, a surly, "Because, Ms. Radu, you should not have left something like this until the last minute."

Sabina flipped the man the bird as she stomped out of the office and headed to the women's changing room, for the mandatory, and in her view unnecessary, prerequisite which had to be borne before she could do her job.

She entered the room, and hung up her backpack from which she removed a set of drab-green scrubs and placed them on the bench under her bag.

Stripping out of her clothes, she grumbled to the empty shower stall, "I can understand showering *after* I am done, but before? Is the American afraid I am going to infect his precious dead body with the common cold and kill it more?"

Shaking her head, Sabina adjusted the water temperature and stepped under spray-head.

Magdalina was relieved when she saw the woman she presumed to be Dr. Williamson's assistant.

It clarified the day and time, and affirmed that Dr. Williamson was returning shortly to continue his examination of her body. She smirked, imagining his expression when presented with the puddle of what looked like pig-swill.

Magdalina tailed the woman from a reasonable distance, and watched her enter something, according to the miniature banner on the door, entitled *Female Changing Room* — although what these females were changing into, she preferred not to know.

Cautiously, Magdalina followed, listening to Sabina express her opinion of the current situation.

Unfortunately for the grad student intern, it would be the last thing she ever did.

Magdalina's enhanced vision enabled her to see the pulsing of the woman's carotid artery, sparking an animalistic hunger. The new vampire was not ready to feed, but she had yet to learn to control her bloodlust and could not deny herself so ripe an opportunity.

Relieved to note the water spurting from a metal disc, drowned out her approach, she swooped on her meal with the stealth of a hawk, seizing the woman — who had no chance to identify her attacker — in an iron grip.

As with Enache, Magdalina clenched her arms and legs around her victim's body.

Fangs sank into the throat of naked woman who fought to dislodge Magdalina. Failing, she tried to scream for help, but Magdalina overwhelmed her, siphoning her blood in great mouthfuls.

Unlike Enache, the woman's blood tasted sweeter, redolent of the finest wines her vintner had aged in her cellars, and it slowed Magdalina's heartbeat, momentarily sedating her.

The pair crumpled to the tiles, Magdalina not slackening her hold. The shower's powerful jets swilled any dark red essence not consumed, down the drain.

Mindful of her violent reaction to her own blood when she rid the world of Dr. Enache, she avoided mopping her face and mouth with her hands.

Ignoring her latest repast, Magdalina stepped under the stream of water to rinse the remnants of Sabina Radu from her body. It was reminiscent of the waterfall near the fortress; a place where Cristoff and she had often cleansed themselves during the warmer months.

This chance to indulge in a proper wash was an unexpected luxury. Even though she had been sealed in an airtight sarcophagus at the bottom of the Danube, a thousand years without a bath left a person a trifle... dusty.

With no clue how to stop the spray, Magdalina left it running. Stepping away from the deluge, she squeezed the excess water out of her hair. Glancing around, she plucked the drying sheet from where her victim had hooked it.

Which drew her gaze to the body of Sabina Radu.

Drained of her life force, the corpse was pale and drawn. Her blonde hair, disheveled from the struggle.

The water had removed the evidence of Magdalina's ambush, but she was left with the problem of disposing of the woman's remains.

A thought occurred to her.

If the cooler is good enough for one dead body... why not two?

She purloined the breaches and smock the woman had hung next to the stall, no doubt to be worn once she was cleansed.

"She no longer requires them," Magdalina remarked flippantly.

The vaguely masculine garb flummoxed her. *How do I clothe myself? The last time I dressed, I was assisted by at least one maid.*

The riddle of the apparel. She stifled a giggle, aware she might be ever-so slightly hysterical.

In the end, she followed her instincts and hoped for the best.

On the bench underneath, she spotted something in a dull-green material. It turned out to be two items made from a fabric which felt similar to the white coat.

Magdalina held them out, puzzled by their purpose but, Ms. Radu had brought them here, which meant they were intended to be worn.

Pursing her lips, she shrugged into them. "What a disagreeable combination. Not at all conducive to ease of movement. I never imagined being grateful I have not eaten lately." She chuckled, then gave an experimental wriggle, willing the clothing to settle more comfortably.

Eventually, believing she looked presentable, Magdalina checked her appearance in the floor length mirror, and nodded her approval, unaware she was wearing everything inside out.

Dressed… after a fashion… the vampire dragged the body from the shower. Hefting it over her shoulder like the kill from a hunt, she retraced her steps to the morgă.

Magdalina paused when she reached the door, certain she had left it open when she snuck out. *How did it close on its own?*

Unnerved, she strained her ears for any indication she was not alone. *Did someone else shut it?*

Blessed silence.

Has the damnable dragon enchanted the entrances in this structure?

Baffled, she tried the handle. Nothing. It was as locked as Williamson's had been. Adding to her confusion, the mechanism on *this* door was different… in fact, she could not even locate it.

Exasperated, Magdalina shrugged the body from her shoulder, and propped it against the wall in order to examine the door more closely. The only object she could find was a thin black and silver box jutting out of the wall next to the frame with a slim groove at one edge.

Frowning, she contemplated the folly of her endeavor. *Evidently, this door lacks a key…*

The thought trailed off as she recalled something from the note, she had seen on Williamson's table.

…her key…

She muttered a curse, realizing it was in a pouch of the

white coat-like garment she had acquired in the morgă, and discarded in the changing room.

Running back to the room, now engulfed in steam from the unattended shower, Magdalina wasted several minutes checking the movable storage bins before locating the one containing the item in question.

Rifling through the pockets, she recovered the magical rectangle.

Dashing out, Magdalina skidded across the wet tiles, thanks, in part, to a second rectangle which Sabina had, unknowingly, dropped on the floor.

Picking it up, Magdalina squinted at it through the steam. Similar to the one she already possessed, this one did not display the image of Sabina Radu.

Something told her, she ought to keep it.

Returning to the morgue, Magdalina's eyes swung between the sealed door, for any slot the 'key' might fit, and the corridor, for any approaching guard.

Aware she was running out of options, and time, Magdalina slid the card over the surfaces of the door and the frame, to no avail.

On the verge of abandoning the body, she took a step back to study the puzzling protrusion next to the doorframe. The slit at the right hand edge, pulled at her resourceful brain.

By sheer dumb luck, Magdalina slid the card along the crevice in the correct manner, rewarded with a soft *snick*.

Whatever sorcery the dragon might have employed to keep her out, had ceded its control and granted her access.

Thanking the sprite which must be living in the rectangle,

Magdalina hauled her victim off the floor and entered the room before the magical creature changed its mind.

Deciding to put Ms. Radu in the same drawer as the doctor's remains, she hurried to the bank of shiny doors, opening the one containing Enache.

It looks big enough for two.

A thought struck her. *Why waste a corpse? I doubt anyone will be able to distinguish one cadaver from another, especially one in Sabina Radu's condition.*

She knew Williamson was going to perform something he had referred to as an autopsy on her body, but had no clue what that entailed.

"Perhaps the man intends to conduct some sort of necromancy. Better you than me, peasant," Magdalina muttered.

Whatever had awaited her, and now Ms. Radu, Magdalina presumed it involved the rolling table, on which Williamson had laid her when she first arrived.

Scanning the room, she noticed two more identical tables in one corner.

Daringly she peeked under the white sheets covering the strange humps to find two skeletons, intrigued as to their history, rather than aghast by the distorted and shattered bones.

Although saddened by the barbarity of their deaths, she could do no more for them, and attended to Ms. Radu.

Hefting the body onto the table originally assigned to her, Magdalina arranged it as best she could. She located a fresh white sheet from one of the cupboards, draped it over the remains, and wheeled the table to where the other two stood.

"There you go, Doctor Williamson, your aberrant activity awaits."

Satisfied, Magdalina went in search of somewhere safe to take a nap.

Chapter Six

Sunday Morning
9:00 AM

Dr. Christopher Williamson was beside himself as he stood in front of his office with one end of a door knob in his hand. He was even more flabbergasted when his supposedly locked door swung open.

Without hesitating, he charged in and began an inventory of his relics.

While he doubted anyone would be able to decipher the writings, the age of the scrolls and the manuscripts was enough to garner a fair price from a collector on the black market.

He cursed himself for not securing his antiquities under a sturdier lock and key.

Looking up from his desk, he saw a security guard in the doorway.

"Nicolescu, were you on duty last night?" Williamson barked.

Surprised the person knew his name, the guard — a

recent appointee at the Institute — did not recognize the speaker, nor did he understand English, although he *did* register the American accent from the occasional news report he had seen on television.

Concerned as to the validity of the man's presence, Nicolescu ordered in Romanian, "Halt or I'll contact the police."

Williamson smacked himself in the forehead with the palm of his hand, realizing the communication gaffe.

He took a breath and replied in the same language, "Please do. It appears someone has broken into my office and may have stolen some of my work. Literature vital to my research."

"That cannot be." The guard jutted out his chin defensively. "I checked your office on my rounds and saw no intruders. Perhaps you are mistaken."

"Mistaken?" Williamson growled. "Get out of here and summon the police, otherwise, I might toss your worthless ass through the window."

Nicolescu exited the crazy American's office with alacrity.

Explains why the world hates them so much, he grumbled inwardly.

At the corner, on his way to the security station at the end of the adjoining passage, the guard looked back to see the doctor disappearing into the morgue.

He thought nothing of it and carried on, until an anguished screech reverberated throughout the facility.

It was a hopeless cry, the likes of which the guard had never heard. Debating whether to investigate, he decided against it and quickened his pace.

The blare of the klaxon, sent the bulk of the security detail scrambling to the morgue.

Swept up in the stampede, the guard had no choice but to follow.

The squad entered the morgue to be met by a rancid smell, which stalled their advance. Too late for the first sentry through the door, who promptly fainted dead away, hitting the floor with a solid *thud.*

The remainder stood transfixed by the scene, none wanting to approach any closer.

Nicolescu saw the doctor standing next to an open door on the cooler wall. Dripping from the body tray… in shades of black and red… a putrid, viscous mess, globs of which were splattering onto the floor.

Clenched in Williamson's fist, a crudely carved wooden spike.

The American demanded, "Where is that bastard Enache? He is responsible for this, I know it. He will answer for this catastrophe. Find him."

Bemused by Williamson's wild accusations against the man most had known from the first days of their employment, the guards failed to notice the woman in scrubs weaving through the group.

She elbowed past them, pausing long enough to see the stupefied expression on Williamson's face.

Without missing a beat, she crossed to one of the tables in the corner. All eyes focused on her as she lifted the sheet to uncover a corpse… ghastly pale.

As one, the guards inhaled sharply.

Williamson hurried to the table, surveyed the remains, then pinned a curious gaze on the intern.

What the hell was going on here? This was not the cadaver he had removed from the casket. Whoever this was had not been dead for nigh on a thousand years, more like two days.

He strove to maintain his equanimity, suspecting the woman staring at him so innocently… too innocently… was somehow involved, and he intended to ascertain how and to what extent.

She looked as though she had been dressed by a blind-folded donkey... *how many layers? It wasn't that cold in here...* and there were some unsavory-looking smears on her scrubs, which ought to be spotless. *Weren't interns instructed to shower before entering the morgue?*

A broken lock, a disheveled assistant, and a copious amount of bodily fluids for which he could not account. Something very fishy — and not just the nauseating odor permeating the room — was afoot.

On the brink of quizzing the woman regarding this troublesome state of affairs, the question died on his tongue when she spoke first.

In direct but not quite modern Romanian, she asked, "Is there a problem? You are Doctor Williamson are you not? I was ordered to assist him in his *autospy*," she stumbled over the last word, still unsure what it meant.

"If you are not him, I must ask you to leave." Though she already knew who he was. "He is due momentarily, and I daresay he will not appreciate your presence."

"No, yes, I am Doctor Williamson, and you are?"

The woman reached into the pocket of her scrubs and withdrew the card identifying her as Sabina Radu, the one without the image.

Aware she did not resemble the woman on Ms. Radu's official card, Magdalina was glad she had picked up the second one from the floor of the changing room. Handing over the original was akin to confessing she had been in his locked office.

Nevertheless, there was something about him which told her, he could be trusted.

Williamson studied the new intern, who held her breath, speculatively for several seconds.

He seemed to come to a conclusion as, without further ado, he nodded at the metal door. "Any idea what happened there?"

The intern followed his gaze and shrugged, "Poor equipment? Or maybe you should hire a more capable cleaning woman? Whatever the cause, it was in that state when I came to prepare the body for you, as assigned by Doctor Lupu."

Williamson arched a brow at the woman's odd explanation.

"Doctor Williamson…" one of the guards in the group found his voice, "…is there anything you need of us? If not, may we be excused?"

"No, thank you for your swift attendance." Williamson waved them off.

As they trudged out of the morgue, Williamson hailed the guard he had chastised earlier, "Nicolescu, no need to contact the authorities…" glancing across the table at his new assistant, "…it is an old building. No doubt I was too heavy handed with the lock when I shut my office yesterday."

"Did you not charge that some of your paperwork might be missing?" Nicolescu contested.

"No, you were correct, I was mistaken. I found it hidden under a stack of documents on my desk. If you would be so kind as to excuse us, we have much to do. Oh, and please ask someone to organise a replacement door knob."

"Y-yes, sir." Nicolescu left them to it, his opinion of Americans in no way improved.

Alone with the doctor, Magdalina was assailed by Cristoff's scent. It was growing more potent.

"Miss Radu, could you take the number four handle, with

the twenty-two A scalpel, and make a Y-incision so we can begin?" Williamson's question interrupted, and effectively mitigated, the sensory overload inundating Magdalina.

She looked at the collection of gleaming knives spread out across the small table awaiting use.

Why in the name of the most Holy does anyone need so many blades to cut someone open? Magdalina nearly spoke out loud.

"Is there a problem, Miss Radu?"

"N-no, Doctor Williamson," she stuttered.

Scrutinizing the instruments, she spied something etched into the handles. Arabic numerals she had learned as a child in her mathematics lesson. Whispering a long overdue thanks to her tutor for his insistence, she found one bearing a *4*.

Why they were not in Roman script, she was not sure but, to find knives marked this way, made her ruminate over what else in everyday life had changed.

Alongside the blades, a series of, presumably, the afore-mentioned handles; also carved with Arabic numerals. Iden-tifying the one imprinted with *22*, Magdalina realized, they slotted together, creating a larger knife.

With a judicious eye to the blade, Magdalina scanned the body, unclear what Williamson's instructions meant.

A Y-incision? I have split many a man open with my sword in battle, but I had no idea there was a specific name for a type of cut.

Seeing the intern's hesitation, her hand quivering slightly, Williamson queried, "You have performed an autopsy before, Miss Radu?"

"Of course, Doctor Williamson." She flipped the handle to the doctor. "Just not on a body as old and significant as this."

Accepting the scalpel, Williamson huffed, "Fine. Watch closely. I should not have to demonstrate this more than once."

The blade poised, Williamson started from the upper

right tip of the shoulder, followed by a matching incision from the left side. Both cuts ran in a diagonal line to meet at the hollow between the deceased's breasts.

The incision continued vertically down the midline of the body, stopping at the pubis.

While it came as something of a shock to Williamson that his, apparently useless, assistant did not swoon at the sight of the lacerated corpse, what concerned him more was the latter's lack of blood.

Frowning at the skin of the torso peeled back like huge lapels, he flapped his hand at the collection of tools. "Pass me the sternal bone saw."

Fortunately, Magdalina guessed the correct tool this time. Occasionally, she had watched her woodsmen felling trees, and remembered the serrated teeth on the blades, they had classified as saws.

Taking the saw from his assistant, Williamson made short work of breaking through the chest cavity.

He noted the organs had a sickly waxen hue, indicative of massive blood-loss, yet this was not what puzzled him.

His earlier hypothesis was correct. This was no ancient cadaver.

He touched the skin. Even allowing for the time the body had been in the carefully controlled atmosphere of the morgue, it ought to be dry and discolored, and feel like aged parchment.

He thought back to the previous day. Despite his excitement over the discovery, his clinical brain had committed several pertinent facts to memory... as was his habit.

This was not the same corpse, he had removed, so meticulously, from the sarcophagus, which begged the question… *who are you, my dear? For you are not my beloved queen.*

Williamson straightened up and, swallowing the urge to

lambaste himself from the morgue to the Danube and back again, drew a calming breath.

"Okay, Christopher, before you jump to conclusions, start again. You are behaving like a third-rate med student, not a seasoned doctor and, though I do say so myself, experienced archaeologist. Get with the program."

Duly instructed, he commenced a comprehensive inspection, beginning with the largest organ.

The first thing he noticed were the two puncture marks marring an otherwise flawless throat, something he did not expect to find. Odder still, while it was clear the wounds were fresh, they were already in a reparative state, indicating an accelerated healing process... which was, of course, irrational.

"What happened here," he murmured, shrewd eyes assessing the skin.

"H-how should I know," his assistant stammered.

Startled, his gaze met her wary one. "Damn, I'm sorry. I totally forgot you were there."

"I get that a lot." She blushed.

"Ok... time to turn her. I wonder..."

There was a pause, while Williamson rolled the body over.

He frowned and straightened up, his mind whirling.

"It's not there..." a quiet voice intruded.

"And what might that be?" he challenged, a slight edge to his tone.

"I am under the impression you know what you are looking for. The birthmark is not there."

"Birthmark?"

The intern pivoted slowly, and tweaked the neckline of her clothing to expose a rose-hued blemish on the top of her left shoulder blade.

To anyone else, it would appear as nothing more than a

scar from a childhood injury. To those who knew better, it was a family mark. An ugly reminder of a deed inflicted on an unknowing bloodline.

"Perhaps we ought to terminate this pointless exercise and adjourn to my office. I do believe a discussion regarding this... turn of events is in order, and I prefer we not be disturbed," Williamson suggested.

The woman sized him up across the table and took her courage in both hands.

"On one condition. Tell me where to find Cristoff."

"In good time... my queen."

Chapter Seven

E scorting Magdalina to his office, Williamson closed and locked the newly repaired door behind them.

Magdalina shuffled her feet, in much the same way as she had when reprimanded by her tutor either for failing to complete her studies on time or permitting Cristoff to copy her work.

"Please, make yourself comfortable," Williamson invited, pulling a shabby chair to the front of his desk.

Circling the large and battered piece of furniture, still buried under the various manuscripts Magdalina had perused, he settled into his own chair.

Neither spoke, and a curious hush descended on the room.

Williamson rummaged through the pile, documents sliding dangerously close to the edge of his desk.

Magdalina, who had no idea for what he sought, remained standing behind the proffered seat, staring at him, nonplussed.

"If you know who I am, why are you not afraid of me, of

what I have become?" Magdalina ventured, no longer able to bear the quiet.

Finding the document, he wanted from under the pile, Williamson was busy scribbling something at the bottom of the sheet. The question jerked his attention back to the woman.

Folding his arms, he sucked on the inside of his mouth as though considering his words carefully.

The longer Williamson took to respond, the more Magdalina began to fidget, glad the chair blocked his view of her legs.

"Say something," she demanded.

With a sigh, he confessed, "Because I have been compelled to spend thirteen lifetimes atoning for my failure to protect you, Queen Magdalina."

Magdalina's jaw dropped. There was no polite description for her stunned reaction.

"P-pray, might you repeat that very, very slowly," she croaked, gripping the back of the chair, her nails scoring the strange material.

Williamson gave a lop-sided smile and did as she asked, adding, "I was beginning to think you were lost to me forever."

"H-how… w-why… b-but… i-if…"

Magdalina shook her head and coerced her recalcitrant tongue to do her bidding. "When they sealed me in that sarcophagus, they threw your heart in beside me. How can you be here, now, alive? How did you know you were he, he was you? Oh…"

Magdalina's legs threatened to buckle, and her mind reeled with the revelation.

Seeing her sway, Williamson — or was he truly Cristoff?…her heart fluttered — sprang to his feet and was beside her in a flash, to guide her gently onto the chair.

Seated, she twisted her fingers in her lap, uncharacteristically lost for words. Her troubled gaze met Williamson's solicitous one. She studied him, seeking that which ought to be apparent.

Eyes of forest green; she recollected them twinkling with amusement or darkening with ardor. Unruly black hair, which refused to be confined in a cue, now threaded with hints of gray. Angular features, not particularly handsome but imposing. A noble face, a warrior's face.

The drumming of her heart increased and heat spiraled along her veins as images of their clandestine passion reared in her mind. With an effort, she suppressed them.

Not yet...

Williamson was watching her, meditatively.

Has he forgotten my... attributes?

Magdalina smiled hesitantly.

"I need to comprehend this extraordinary proclamation. How are you, a man of the," his condemnation of Enache came back to her, "twentieth century?" She looked at him for confirmation. He nodded. *"Twentieth century.* I have been entombed for a millennium...?" she trailed off, the ramifications of this knowledge too huge to assimilate.

Changes, advances, improvements, and inventions. The births and deaths. Invasions, shifting frontiers, wars. Her mind boggled.

The few innovations, she had seen while navigating this labyrinth of a building were confronting enough. Now she had to contend with a whole world, conceivably altered beyond recognition. Could she... *would she...* survive?

His words came back to her. *I have been compelled to spend thirteen lifetimes atoning for my failure to protect you, Queen Magdalina.*

"If you are indeed my liegeman, what happened?" She narrowed her eyes, waiting.

A shadow passed over Williamson's features. "I was struck from behind, run through by the sword of a coward. My last memory... your tears on my face."

Magdalina sucked in a pained breath. Only he would know that last detail. Seconds later he was dragged from her arms, his body desecrated.

"According to folklore, your betrayers and their men ensured..." Cristoff started, only to fall silent.

The tragic expression which had distorted the beautiful face, he knew so well, still haunted him. Further elaboration was unnecessary and, to evoke the horrors of that day, an unwarranted cruelty.

"Cristoff..." her forlorn wail echoed across a thousand years.

"My Queen," he stood and bowed, the chivalrous gesture, eliciting a flurry of memories.

"This... this..." she faltered. "How can you be him? Are you like me...?"

Magdalina was not ready to name the abomination she had become... *a vampiress*, her mind whispered... or that it required her to feast on human blood.

Who on earth would find that *an endearing trait? Certainly not one who might become a victim to her prodigious appetite.*

"It is a long story, but one I believe you will find absorbing, if rather convoluted." He smiled, his slow sweet smile. When he did that, he could tell her the moon was a stuffed boar and she would believe him.

His scent, which earlier had left her teetering like an inebriated cow-herder, now steadied her, grounded her, suffused her with much needed, and long-lost stamina. Oddly, it was not the same as the energy which permeated her body after slaking her bloodlust. This was more cerebral than physical.

"It appears I have until the end of the world and then

some." She sighed. "I confess I am somewhat discomposed by... everything. I feel as though I am walking through the sinking sand at the edge of the marshes. Everything is unbalanced and nothing is as I remember."

"I wish I could alleviate your distress, my queen, but perhaps if we focus on my discoveries, it will diminish." Cristoff suggested encouragingly.

"What do I have to lose?"

Chapter Eight

"Throughout my thirteen lifetimes, I have scoured the earth for evidence of your resting place and anything pertaining to the curse which, reputedly, you broke the morning of the battle—" Cristoff started.

"I saw your manuscripts, these manuscripts." She indicated the collection scattered across the desk.

"These are a mere handful. I have many more."

He rose and walked to a tall cupboard. Retrieving a key from the inside pocket of his jacket, he unlocked it and opened the door, revealing shelves stacked with all manner of documents from papyrus to parchment to great leather bound books.

Magdalina was by his side before the thought formulated in her head, her fingers itching to examine each one. "How did you find all these?" she murmured reverently.

"This is my penance." He shrugged, almost shyly. "To find you, however long it took."

"I fail to understand why you are being punished for something beyond your control."

Magdalina was baffled by his assertion that, somehow, he

was responsible for her capture and death. "You protected me until you were cut down. What more could you have done?"

"Dragged you kicking and screaming out of that damned fortress, by the hair if need be, until you were out of harm's way."

"A laudable if ignominious, to me at least, impulse. Even had you succeeded, our enemies were tenacious. To permit me to escape was unconscionable. They would never stop hunting me. Sooner or later, they would have achieved their aim."

"I did not believe that, my queen, but…" he paused.

"But what?"

Cristoff hesitated, unwilling to articulate what he had learned. In this clinical office, surrounded by modern technology, it sounded ridiculous.

"Cristoff, what is it?"

"The legend."

"I broke the pledge and transformed it into a curse," Magdalina said. "I mocked the dragon. It was my fault you died. I lost faith."

Cristoff, who could describe all of his lifetimes, in detail, and had investigated numerous myths associated with demons — attested to by the swath of documents — was torn between affirming her contention and dismissing it as poppycock.

Most of what he had unearthed, turned out to be nothing more than a way for power-hungry leaders to keep their followers from straying.

Fear was a stronger motivator than faith. A lesson he had learned too well.

His research to date, pointed to a single source for the multiple demons peppering the historical record which, over time, had been commandeered by different races, creeds, and religions, twisted, and exaggerated to suit individual philosophies.

He explained this to Magdalina, who deliberated over his reasoning.

"Does this mean there is not, there never was, a curse. There must be, for how else am I here eons after I ought to be naught but bones?"

"My practical, scientific mind says yes, but there are things I have read which counter that perspective, never mind my personal history. I would prefer to err on the side of caution. If we discount the curse, you… we… may be vulnerable to the consequences."

"I have heard the dragon in my head. Taunting me, declaring I betrayed him, that my debt can never be paid." Magdalina's startling blue eyes shimmered with unshed tears. "Because I corrupted his covenant, my punishment is eternal servitude."

"Unless we uncover a way to nullify the curse."

"How?" Magdalina opened her palms, helplessly.

"The answer lies here, somewhere." Cristoff waved his hand at the piles of collated evidence.

"We go back to the beginning and review everything?" Magdalina's sharp mind caught on quickly. "If nothing else, I will be blessed to peruse those exquisite manuscripts."

Being a Sunday, the institute was quieter than the morgue along the corridor.

The only sound in Williamson's office was the swish of papers being shuffled or the scratching of a pen as notes were made. Cristoff took gleeful delight in demonstrating the new-fangled writing implements to Magdalina who was mesmerized.

"To secrete ink within the quill is miraculous." Her amazement, palpable.

"It is a pen, and the ink comes in many colors. The choice and type of instrument is vast." Cristoff grinned at her astonishment, picking up a thinner utensil with a gray point at one end.

"This is a pencil and can be erased… removed… by this item." He indicated a small off-white rectangular block made of a strange compressible material. "Then there are crayons, highlighters, and markers, to name but a few."

Opening the top drawer of his desk, he displayed his collection.

Magdalina stared, curiosity tempting her to try every last one, common sense dictating she possess her soul with patience.

"I only ever use pencil on manuscripts, and even that is tantamount to blasphemy but I needed to mark certain texts, otherwise trying to recollect where salient information was mentioned would be impossible."

"Fascinating," Magdalina's gaze swung between the cupboard and the desk, her forehead creasing at the enormity of their task. "Where do we start?"

Cristoff went back to the cupboard and removed a pile of rolled documents, carrying them carefully to an adjacent and empty table.

"These are the earliest testimonies. Be careful, the papyrus is incredibly fragile."

Cristoff dragged the two chairs over from the desk, and offered one to Magdalina.

He switched on an overhead light. The beam was as bright as the sun. Magdalina glanced up, squinting against the glare.

"What sorcery creates so brilliant a torch?" she asked, reminded of the similar, although less dazzling, candles in the corridor.

"That is a light and is created by a relatively recent invention known as electricity," Cristoff said, realizing how alien, and probably frightening, the world must appear to a person who lived forty generations before these modern technologies.

"You will be faced with many strange things as you navigate this era, my Queen. The best way to cope is to accept without question, otherwise your head might explode."

"Please, call me Magdalina. I am no longer your queen," she entreated with a rueful smile.

Cristoff retrieved a pair of spectacles and slid them on. He looked at the woman seated so close, he could take her hand and never let go.

"You will always be my queen, but I shall acquiesce to your request."

His formal tone, at odds with the affection glimmering in his arresting green eyes. "Now to work. The day is already half over."

Once Cristoff had explained how he liked to record his findings, Magdalina, conversant with ancient texts, immersed herself in one manuscript after another. It took a few attempts to get the pen to do her bidding, but was soon scribbling notes as rapidly as Cristoff.

Hours passed in what felt like minutes. It did not take Magdalina long to isolate certain terminology, which made it easier to discard unrelated documents without needing to check every line. Some papers were read in detail, others required no more than a cursory glance.

. . .

Cristoff straightened up and flexed his back, aching a little from being hunched over. He removed his specs and pinched the bridge of his nose.

With some surprise he noticed that, apart from where the duo was sitting under the incandescent light, the room was in shadow. He checked his watch. The hand on the dial glowed faint green.

6:30.

He put down his pen. "Time to go home. No sense in trying to do it all in one go."

Placing her pen alongside his, Magdalina stretched her arms above her head… a mistake given the mental image it induced. She dropped them quickly, flinching when her muscles protested.

She did not ask the obvious.

Where am I supposed to go? I have no castle, not even a bed. What about sustenance? Will my stomach accept food or am I consigned to draining unsuspecting victims for the rest of my existence?

She regarded Cristoff who was clearing the table, putting the piles of papers they had worked through onto three separate shelves in the cupboard.

He caught her gaze. "Of no use, some helpful information, vital evidence." Pointing at each shelf as he spoke.

Magdalina nodded absently, her mind veering off on a tangent. *What about this man? Do I address him as Cristoff or Williamson?*

Her head was spinning. Too many questions and not enough answers.

"Something amiss?" he pried, removing an oblong box from the cupboard, which he tucked into his backpack.

Her nose crinkled. "I am at a loss. What should I do? Is there a bed in this… this… strange fortress?"

Registering her predicament, Cristoff, ensuring everything was secured properly, suggested tentatively, "Perhaps you might consider accompanying me to my residence. It is modest but comfortable, and I will arrange dinner once we get there."

"You would permit me to sleep in your abode?"

"Of course, should you deem it suitable."

"I have been sleeping in a coffin for a thousand years," she countered drily. "The floor of a stable would seem luxurious by comparison."

Shouldering his backpack, Cristoff chuckled. "In that case, my Queen..." he crooked his elbow invitingly. "Keep that ID card, the one you took from Ms. Radu," he clarified at Magdalina's bewilderment. "It will prevent awkward questions."

His concern about awkward questions led to another, "I know you have taken pains to affirm you are my Cristoff, but everyone here refers to you as Doctor Williamson. Do you prefer I address you as such?"

Magdalina blushed, this reversal of their ranks, disconcerting.

She used to be the one in control, the one with the authority. Now she was flailing, as though a rug had been pulled out from under her.

Cristoff mulled that over, before chuckling.

"My given name is Christopher, but among my friends I'm known as Chris, a respectable abbreviation." He jogged his elbow again.

Despite being a queen in her own time, Magdalene was unsure whether accepting his arm was appropriate, given their complicated circumstances.

She assumed Chris... *that name would take some adjusting to...* was unlikely to behave in a manner contrary to etiquette.

Shyly, she slid her hand around his arm, her fingers coming to rest on his sleeve.

Cristoff switched off the light, plunging the room into darkness. The pair exited into the equally dim corridor, and Chris escorted Magdalina to the staff entrance.

Chapter Nine

D r. Williamson's dwelling lay in the heart of old Bucharest.

Founded in 1459, by none other than the infamous ruler or *voivode* of Wallachia, Vlad Tepes, the city was unknown to Magdalina.

While Cristoff thought his companion would relish the story of Vlad the Impaler — whose father was known as *The Dragon* in his time — it was a tale for another night.

Magdalina stood agape at the size of the fortress where Cristoff lived.

"I-Is this yours?" she asked, spellbound. Another example of how dramatically their roles were reversed. "You said you were comfortable, but not even I could have afforded such an extravagant palace. Does everyone enjoy this opulence?"

"Hardly, and this is not opulent. I have an apartment, one of many dwellings within the shell of this structure," he demurred, grinning.

"Oh." Magdalina nodded as though she understood what he meant. "This building is similar to an inn?"

"Sure, we can go with that."

Cristoff ushered her into something he tagged an elevator.

Magdalina, pressing her lips together to curb the babbling terror the contraption elicited, dispensed with decorum and clutched his arm for grim death, certain, at any moment, the flying cage would pitch them to their deaths.

Only when they reached the safety of the third floor, which Cristoff stated was the level on which he lived, did she relax her grip, reverting to her usual insouciance — to Cristoff's well-concealed amusement.

Entering the frugal but attractively furnished apartment, Cristoff said, "I'm going to order delivery. Feel free to explore."

Dubious about whether ordering a priest to deliver them from evil was worth the coin, Magdalina did not question it and, instead, ventured out onto the narrow balcony.

She was held motionless at the splendor of the settlement, spread out as far as the eye could see, and bathed in the glow of what she presumed to be the same type of illumination, Cristoff had in his office.

Inhaling deeply, she savored the aroma of food being prepared below. Her stomach rumbled, reminding her of what she was.

Am I still able to eat actual food?

Time would tell.

She went back inside, and wandered the room, drawn to a set of wooden shelves which contained a veritable cornucopia of books and yet more manuscripts.

As she withdrew a volume with an uncommonly shiny cover, another caught her eye, prompting her to place the newer tome on the little table beside one of the chairs.

Unlike the rest of the collection, this one had no writing on the bound spine. Sliding it from the shelf, she noted it was battered, and somewhat water damaged. The leather cover was stiff with age, and creaked alarmingly when she opened it. The pages were parchment or perhaps vellum and, even though yellowed, were of excellent quality. This was a costly item.

It fell open near the back and, turning the pages with gentle fingers, she realized it was written in Cristoff's hand, using one of those magical pens.

She sank onto one of the cozy chairs and began to read.

26 February, 1937
Heir Himmler has granted permission and provided adequate funding, for me to search for my queen's sarcophagus. He believes the legends surrounding her disappearance, and agrees that to find it would give Hitler an insurmountable advantage over his enemies.
Something about an army of vampires.
God save us if one side is deranged enough to fire the first shot. Have they learned nothing from the Great War?

Delving deeper into the writings toward the end of the manuscript, she came across a disturbing entry.

1 September, 1939
The fools crossed into Poland today. War across Europe is assured. Hopefully, Romania will remain neutral so I may continue my research.

20 November, 1940
Our puppet king was ordered by his corrupt prime minister to declare support for the Nazi's. We are ill-prepared for war and it will be only a matter of time before the Bolsheviks reach our doorsteps.

23 August, 1944

*War makes strange bedfellows. King Micheal has cut his tether to
PM Antonescu and has finally decided to throw his hat in with the
Allies.*
Even the madman in Berlin is aware the war is all but over.
*Word has come down from German High Command to destroy all
the treasures they have spent the last ten years stealing.*
My heart cannot allow such a disaster to occur.

1 September, 1944
*The Russians are poised to enter the country seeking whatever
spoils of war they can seize. I expect Stalin will sell what he can to
the highest bidder to recoup a portion of the cost of the war.*
*I have spent the last week in a valiant attempt to save the most
priceless pieces. I plan to smuggle them out of Romania aboard a
Nazi river boat, praying I will be intercepted by either the Americans or the British west of Vienna.*
May God grant me success.

This part of the story captivated Magdalina. The Cristoff
she knew had little appreciation for the arts. He considered
them a frivolity for the rich.

Here, though, her liegeman had risked his life for the sake
of painting and sculptures.

Reaching the last page of the book, her eye was drawn to
a wine-colored blotch. Long since dry, Magdalina detected
the scent of blood.

2 September, 1944
0026
*We have departed Giurgiu docks and are heading up river. The
vessel is weighed down with artifacts, but I had to leave behind an
equal amount.*
*A travesty, but to delay any longer would risk capture by the
Germans, the partisans, or the Russians.*

I cannot be sure the Western Allies will be in Vienna, when we arrive. It is in God's hands now.

0130
The sound of propellers can be heard approaching from the east. It is too dark to distinguish the air force to which it belongs.

0139
They have opened fi

The entry went unfinished. A bloodstain its punctuation.

Some of the terminology eluded her, but the essence of the passages was crystal clear.

A ringing sound caused her to snap the book closed and tuck it between herself and the chair.

She glanced up.

Cristoff was setting two bags on the large table between the kitchen and dining room... an unconventional but, in Magdalina's opinion, practical joining of the two spaces, which, in her fortress had been two floors and several corridors apart.

"I see you found my library." He nodded at the book on the table.

"Library? I had better collections of manuscripts in fire gutted monasteries."

Cristoff brushed off Magdalina's slight, spotting what she was attempting to hide.

"Ahhh, my journal."

"A journal? Is that the title of this peculiar form of manuscript?"

"Aye. And this one is unique. I bought it in London..."

hmmm, sometime around eighteen-hundred... it was so long ago, I've forgotten the exact date.

"Since then, whenever one life ended, I'd find it in the same quaint London bookshop from where I originally purchased it, in the next. The Wise Owl on Old Compton Street. I'll take you there one day."

"Is that what happened after...?" she started, then paused.

He did not need it spelling out. "Curiously, no. I found it aboard one of the Nazi riverboats, my team dredged up from the bottom of the Danube, not very long ago."

This prompted another, more delicate question, but Magdalina was not quite sure how to phrase it without sounding insensitive.

The two skeletons in the room of the dead. Until now, she had not put two and two together.

She had no need to voice her suspicion, her queer expression was eloquent enough.

"Yes, one of those sets of partial remains in the morgue was me. Have to admit, it's a bit unnerving to see yourself in that condition."

Magdalina's reply, a candid, "Trust me, I am the last person you need to convince, and what of the treasures you gave your life to save?"

The look on Cristoff's face was one of failure. Paintings by Grand Masters from the Renaissance to Neoclassicism, reduced to waterlogged canvases. Sculptures, bronze and marble, some dating from antiquity, riddled with bullets. The numerous and irreplaceable artifacts scattered across the muddy bottom of the river had broken his heart.

On the plus side, the handful of items he *had* recovered, relatively intact, allowed him to return the following year to investigate the LiDAR anomaly on the riverbed which revealed itself to be Magdalina's final resting place.

Right now, hunger overrode nostalgia.

"Perhaps we can put all things… archaeology related aside for a while. Time for dinner. I ordered some of the local favorites. Are you able to…" he hesitated.

Magdalina was no ordinary woman on a date, she was neither human nor ghost.

His research, not to mention countless books, tv shows, and movies was contradictory, but the consensus inferred that vampires… if this was what Magdalina had become… could only consume blood.

Magdalina shrugged. "I do not know. This is new to me too."

Her impish smile revealed a hint of the carefree girl he had fallen in love with. "I can only try."

"Okay, let me get some plates." He gathered crockery from a cupboard and a handful of metal implements from a drawer in the kitchen.

Arranging them neatly on the table, he indicated, "Plate, bowl, knife…"

Earning a snort from his dinner guest.

"I know what those are. I have only been buried since the twelfth century, not the beginning of time."

Ignoring her, he picked up two utensils, "...fork and spoon."

The former, Magdalina had never seen before; the design of the latter, not wholly unfamiliar.

"I can't have you stabbing yourself in the mouth with the fork, accidentally… or the knife for that matter… while eating. Not sure, I could stem the bleeding."

She winced, recalling the mess in the morgue with the old doctor. "Yes, it would not be a pretty sight."

He lifted a small, white, handle-less bucket from one of the bags and removed the lid. Steam coiled out, to tease the taste buds. He poured equal amounts into the two dishes.

"This is Ciorba Radauteana. It is a soup, like a broth,"

Chris explained. "Made with chicken, and various vegetables, and flavored with garlic and lemon. Elena adds a little spice to give it a kick. Try it. It's delicious."

He chose the thing he had called a spoon, and used it to scoop up some of the liquid.

Blowing, to cool it slightly, he swallowed a mouthful.

"Go on." He nodded at Magdalina's dish. "I speak the truth."

He took another spoonful as though to prove his point.

Even as he appeared to enjoy the *soup*, a single word crawled through her brain... ***poisoned***.

Greatly daring, and glad to see Cristoff was not writhing on the floor in agony, Magdalina dipped her spoon in the creamy soup, testing the temperature with the tip of her tongue. Confident it would not scald, she risked a taste.

Initially it seemed bland, a fact she was about to bemoan when the spice tickled the back of her throat.

She could not repress a mewl of delight. "Cristoff, this is ambrosial."

She emptied her bowl perhaps more quickly than was prudent, her stomach rebelling against the unexpected invasion.

By sheer effort of will, she quashed the threatening regurgitation, but deduced it might be sensible to moderate her enthusiasm.

"You okay?" Chris asked, noting her greenish pallor.

"What is this 'okay'?" Magdalina replied, needing him to distract her until her innards settled.

"Sorry, I keep forgetting. It is a colloquialism, a popular word and has several meanings depending on context," Chris tried to define the term which had become a catch-all.

"If you say, 'I'm okay', it means 'I am fine', or 'I am in good health'. It also means something is acceptable or of a good standard. It can express permission... instead of saying yes, people say okay. It can also denote that something is commonplace."

Magdalina gawped at him.

"That does not help at all." She grimaced. "I suspect it will take me some considerable time to understand this world."

"Wait until you see a television," Chris tried to lighten the moment. "That will blow your mind."

"Blow my mind?"

"Shock you."

Magdalina blew a weary sigh. "Mayhap I ought to be returned to my coffin. That was, at least, uncomplicated."

"You are not serious?" Perturbed, Chris stared at her.

"I know you have lived thirteen lives, which must be confronting, but I never died. I have spent a thousand years on a riverbed, the passage of time both a minute and an eon.

"I have heard the tumult of war and the silence of peace, but have had no need to deal with the changes being wrought above my head.

"It is like being caught in a swirling tempest. Just when I think I am gaining a foothold, I am knocked over. Worse, I have to come to terms with this unnatural immortality, the demon's curse."

For the second time since her deliverance, she felt the sting of tears. After so long as a dry husk, she did not think she had the capacity to cry. Determined not to give into such feminine nonsense, she blinked them back.

Attuned to her every emotion, Chris came around to where she was sitting and, taking her hand, pulled her upright.

"Do not fret, my queen, we shall overcome these challenges together. I am here, and have no intention of leaving you to fend for yourself."

He brushed his lips to her forehead, it was barely a touch,

soft as a butterfly's wing, but Magdalina felt it and the warmth it kindled.

Involuntarily, her arms went around him, she fitted herself to his burly frame, her body recognizing its long lost mate.

"Kiss me, Cristoff," she murmured. "Bring me back to life."

The rest of the food went cold.

Chapter Ten

The pair sequestered themselves from the rest of humanity, splitting their time between Cristoff's cozy Bucharest apartment and the sterile chill of the Institute.

Initially, they continued the façade of finishing the examination of the substitute corpse, during which Magdalina admitted to murdering Dr. Enache, astounded when Chris reacted with nothing more than a perfunctory shrug of his shoulders.

Her surprise was compounded when she discovered muscle memory had returned to her hand enabling her to wield a scalpel with the same dexterity as she had a sword when queen.

Once the *autopsy* was complete and *findings* recorded, they spent every moment Chris was not required elsewhere, rifling through the endless myths, searching for the identity of the demon.

As the days flew by, and aware Magdalina was still recovering... for want of a better description... from her protracted confinement, Chris felt it essential to intersperse the hours of concentration with some light relief.

Afternoon walks offered some respite, but the autumnal air was too brisk for protracted outdoor exercise.

To this end, he introduced his queen to the delights of television.

Unwilling to give Magdalina apoplexy, he tried to demystify the appliance, which had the opposite effect.

"Okay, how about I switch it on and let you ask me questions? That might be easier," he proposed.

Magdalina grasped his hand and squeezed her eyes shut. "Do it quickly," she entreated.

"It will not hurt you," he assured and, disentangling his fingers, crossed the room to the *television* and turned a round knob on the front.

The machine blinked to life.

The sound emanating from the squat box made Magdalina jump, and she peeked through half-closed lids at the images.

Astonished, her eyes flew open and she squawked.

"What is this magic?" Stunned, she forgot to breathe. *People, scenery, and animals inside something so small. How did they get there?*

"I cannot underst…" and, unable to help herself, walked around to check behind the box. Her brows knitted. This was incredible.

"Now might be a good time to put that whole 'accept without questioning' into practice," Cristoff said, placidly. He turned the knob at the other side and a different scene filled the glass.

"Each one of these is a channel, I am lucky enough to be able to access two, and there are several different programs. Some tell us about the state of the world, some are dedicated to leisure activities, and some are just for fun." He thought this was the least complicated way to illustrate the differences between the stations.

Since the collapse of communism… something Magdalina neither knew nor cared about… the viewing options and broadcasting hours were slowly increasing but, sometimes, this present-day Chris really missed the variety of shows available on American television.

Riveted by the invention, Magdalina did not answer.

Thus began her obsession with television. Along with the journal, and the mouthwatering meals, Chris served, it became a highlight of her day.

Keenly aware their priority was identifying a method of dispatching the dragon, permanently, *not* indulging in this form of entertainment… however impressive… she *did* manage to limit her time in front of the box until after the evening meal.

Consequently, working separately while comparing their findings, the pair came to the same conclusion.

Supremacy over the dragon lay in deciphering its name.

That dragons even *had* names, seemed spurious but they could not ignore the evidence.

Once that was determined, they should be able to track the demon to its lair, presuming it had one in this century, and begin the process of banishing it to the underworld, freeing the couple once and for all.

While it sounded easy in theory; in reality, it was quite the opposite.

Some manuscripts guaranteed success. Other papyri warned of dire consequences should anyone be stupid enough to attempt such a naive maneuver.

One evening, nearing madness from the interminable contradictions, Magdalina slapped a handful of documents onto the table in disgust, growling, "Why do the so-called scholars not agree; you go to cave X and do Y to kill dragon Z."

She got up to pace the room, her agitation plain.

Cristoff rose from his chair to draw her into a comforting embrace.

Burying her face into his chest, she lamented disconsolately, "I have been here more than two weeks, yet I struggle to comprehend the simplest of things, notwithstanding your best efforts. Even addressing you as Chris sounds foreign to my ears, despite my memories of the nights spent in your arms."

After his first sublime but, to date, only kiss, their relationship had undergone a subtle shift.

They were not lovers, but were more than acquaintances, more than friends.

The passion they once shared, simmered beneath the surface, but neither was ready to succumb to temptation. The chasm of the centuries separating them had not been bridged. It might never be bridged.

They were... almost... content to allow things to unfold spontaneously.

Brushing his lips against her silky hair, Cristoff sought to lighten the mood, "I rather enjoy the diffidence in your voice when you try calling me Chris."

A small but well-toned fist punched his chest.

Extricating herself from his embrace, she pivoted away. Without looking back, she chastised his teasing. "You are a blackguard."

"Maybe so, but I have had a thousand years to practice."

Magdalina stopped in her tracks.

The enormity of what Cristoff or Chris — or whatever name he had gone by since last they met — must have experienced during the last millennium, struck her like a hammer.

I have no clue how he lived, or who he might have lived with, or bedded...

Tears brimmed in her eyes... again, *honestly, I am worse than a watering pot.* Magdalina felt his hands graze her shoulders, but did not want him to see her in this condition.

Hardening her heart, she announced, "I am going to bed."

Cristoff's reply was colored by puzzlement and sadness. "Okay, if that's what you want. Don't forget, I have to leave early in the morning. I am returning to your burial site to finalize the investigation. Would you care to accompany me?"

"I spent enough time beneath those waters," Magdalina shot back. "What makes you think I wish to see it again?"

"I thought perh—" Cristoff began, then, gauging it a waste of breath, opted for, "I'll be away for a few days. Gives you an opportunity to explore the city."

Flinging herself on her bed, Magdalina did something she had not done in longer than she could remember — she cried herself to sleep.

Rising well after the sun, Magdalina crept out of her room to find the apartment empty, just as Cristoff had advised.

On the low table in front of the long cushioned bench, *no... it was a sofa*, she found a small stack of paper he had taught her was the currency of this realm.

She sat down to consider her next move when the annoying voice whispered in her ear, "You know your man lies to you. He is even more of a sweet talking devil than I could ever hope..."

His determination to drive a wedge between Cristoff and her would not succeed.

"Shut up. I am in neither the mood nor have the time to listen to you."

"I am only trying to help you. You suspected the food he gave you the first night might be tainted."

"Thanks to the mistrust you tried to instil within me, accusing Cristoff of feeding me poisoned food."

"It is not mistrust, my dear, it is precaution. You should not place your faith in anyone except me."

"Says the demon who wants me to live off the blood of others like some sadistic parasite."

The dragon ignored her analogy, wheedling, "What of the woman he is using to prepare your meals. You must admit, unless the food is on fire, the taste leaves you dissatisfied, your appetite unassuaged."

"I said, *shut up*!"

"I am curious, when was the last time you fed properly, besides the mess you made of the old man and the wench? You are of royal birth. You should only drink the freshest blood."

Magdalina acknowledged his point, his words stimulating an intense thirst.

"Consider this," the voice crooned persuasively. "If the cook cannot fill you with her food, perhaps she could with her blood."

Withstanding the fierce compulsion to do the demon's bidding, Magdalina retaliated, "B-but what of Cristoff? He will not forgive me for killing his friend."

"Why should that matter? Go!"

Magdalina descended the seemingly endless stairs of the building, preferring that to tempting fate at the hands of the rickety cage.

Safely on the ground floor, she stepped outside and paused, to study her surroundings.

The street was wide, the array of aristocratic buildings, mellow in the October sunlight. The avenue of trees, their leaves gleaming like flaming jewels, heralded the approach of winter. What little she had seen of Bucharest was magnificent.

She breathed in a lungful of the fresh air, on which drifted a heady bouquet leading her to the door of *Elena's Bistro.*

Magdalina guessed 'bistro' was some kind of title which informed people the place served food made by the afore-mentioned Elena. She studied the cheerful colors, and nodded her approval. A clever moniker.

It was too early for the noon meal, and the place seemed empty.

When Magdalina pushed open the door, a bell chimed, making her check above her head and summoning a lady from the rear of the establishment. This must be the Elena of the cooking and the sign.

"Ah, good morning." The woman greeted her unexpected customer with a smile. "I'm Elena..." confirming Magdalina's assumption, "...and I'm afraid you have caught me between services. May I offer you a cup of coffee while I finish my preparations?"

"U-Uh yes, that would be most welcome," Magdalina answered. The exotic spices the woman used in her cooking, intermingled with the scent of her blood drove the vampire to near hysterics, and it was all she could do not to strike.

When Elena set the freshly brewed drink before

Magdalina, however, its fragrance had an extraordinarily calming effect. A small smile of relief spread over her lips.

Hearing a soft chuckle, Magdalina's gaze swung to her server.

"I wish all my customers had the same zen-like expression when handed a cup of my coffee. Most make a funny *ewww* face."

Unsure what the woman meant, Magdalina widened her smile, hoping this was an acceptable reaction, and sipped from the cup. Still vacillating over whether to tear out the woman's throat, a merry voice, followed by the sound of light footsteps, broke her train of thought.

Magdalina saw a small girl of perhaps five or six, skip around the counter separating the rear of the bistro from the dining room. She was a replica of the hostess, in miniature.

"Mama, is Doctor Chris here yet?"

"No, my little lamb. I told you he was going to be out of town for several days."

"*Awwww*." The girl pouted and stomped her small foot. "He promised to bring me a souvenir when he came in next."

"You will just have to be patient," her mother replied, a tinge of reproof in her loving tone.

"Yes, Mama," the girl relented.

"How about saying hello to our guest instead?"

Doe-like eyes shifted to Magdalina, followed by a shy smile and a, "Good morning, ma'am."

"Good morning to you too. Do you know Doctor Chris?"

"Oh yes, he and Papa play cards a lot, though Papa says he is not very good. I am not s'posed to tell Doctor Chris though, or that I think Papa cheats."

The look child sent her Mama was puckish, prompting Elena to shake her head in disbelief at what little eyes saw.

Registering her customer's remark, Elena turned to

Magdalina. "Do you know, Doctor… oh, wait… are you the lady staying with him?"

"Y-yes, for the time being. We are researching an archaeological find he made."

"Please forgive my manners, coffee and lunch are on the house."

Perplexed, Magdalina was at a loss as to how to respond, resisting the temptation to go outside and check the building. *Why would anyone put refreshments on the roof?*

Presuming there might be a linguistic misunderstanding, her customer's Romanian *was* rather peculiar, Elena elucidated, "There is no cost for your food and drink. It is my pleasure to give you this *gratis*.

Cognizant of the Latin for free, Magdalina objected, "No, please, I could not…" she pulled out the small bundle of Romanian Leu, and reassured the woman she could pay.

Elena would not hear of it. "No." She raised her palms, signaling an end to the discussion.

"My place, my rules." She twinkled. "Perhaps you would permit…" She indicated the other chair at the table where Magdalina was sitting.

"I would like that very much," Magdalina, aware this was one argument she was not going to win, acceded.

Elena fetched a cup and a fresh pot of coffee and, as she sat down to join her customer, addressed her daughter, "Magdalina…" startled when the woman sitting across the table replied.

"Yes?"

Two pairs of dark eyes pinned her to the seat.

The little girl squealed, "Is your name Magdalina too?"

Magdalina smiled. "Yes. I was named for my grandmother."

Dragging over a chair, the girl scrambled onto it and — elbows on the table, chin propped on her hands — made it her business to extract every morsel of information from the woman who shared her name.

Giving her very new customer a breather, Elena interposed, "Magda, please run to the kitchen and bring us some pastries."

"The jelly ones, Mama?"

"Yes, the jelly ones too."

As the girl scampered off, Elena fixed Magdalina with a *tell me all the sordid details* expression.

Before getting down to the nitty gritty, she said bluntly, "Chris is a decent bloke. He doesn't do anything without due consideration. So, if you're staying with him, you too must be a good person. Also, I trust my intuition, and I like you. I think we will be friends.

Taking a sip of coffee, Elena, never one to beat about the bush, asked, "Have you slept with the man yet? Lord knows he needs a woman in his life."

Despite the yawning, and for obvious reasons undisclosed, disparity between them in... well... everything, some observations are universal, and the two swapped identical looks of feminine accord.

Their shared mirth obliterated any lingering barriers, and they fell to chattering like magpies.

It was clear to Magdalina why Cristoff enjoyed the company of this family. Watching the child return with a neatly stacked tray of treats, she relished being included, even temporarily.

Vowing she would never divulge to *anyone* how close these two came to becoming fodder for a blood-thirsty monster, Magdalina extinguished the notion, permanently, as Elena invited her to join them for a specially prepared lunch.

"Do you not need to open for business?" Magdalina was concerned for the woman's income.

"Wait, let me check with the boss," Elena said with a grin.

Before the words left her mother's mouth, Magda was nodding furiously, but reminded, "Do not forget, Mama, this day is coming out of your allowance."

"Slave driver," Elena groused, as the trio convulsed with laughter.

Chapter Eleven

Magdalina and her new friend devoured a steaming bowlful of something Elena called *Moldovan Curry*.

"My spin on a traditional stew. I discovered curry on my travels… I was quite the hippy in my youth." She grinned. "I thought a selection would make a great addition to my menu, sets me apart from other restaurants. This is the hottest, on a par with a vindaloo." she explained.

Magdalina did not care that she had not the slightest inkling about hippies or curries or vindaloos. She was in gastronomic heaven. The peppery heat combined with the savoury flavour… utter perfection.

While they were eating, Elena's husband came in. Tall and swarthy, he seemed to fill the room.

His daughter demanded a hug and he swung her into his huge arms, tickling her mercilessly.

"Papa, stop." She chortled.

He put her down and bowed a greeting to the newcomer.

"Vasili, Magdalina. Magdalina, Vasili," Elena introduced.

Magdalina dipped her head in return and remarked how much she was enjoying the dish.

"Pah, he cannot stomach it," Elena taunted her husband who grinned ruefully and patted his belly.

"Ahh, my dear wife is correct. The spice is too much for my delicate constitution." He feigned a grimace and bent to kiss Elena.

"I'll be upstairs," he said to her, adding, "Nice to meet you," to Magdalina."

"Likewise," Magdalina replied with a smile.

Replete, Magdalina felt she ought not impose any longer, aware Elena probably had enough to be doing without entertaining a woman she barely knew.

"Thank you so much, Elena, that was the tastiest meal I have eaten in… oh… an age."

"I remembered Doctor Chris ordered you something spicy on your first night at his apartment. I could hardly pass up the opportunity to share my favorite dish with someone who would actually enjoy it.

"So, you are most welcome, and do not be a stranger. We're open every day, even if you just want to pop in for a coffee and a chat," Elena replied. "I look forward to seeing you soon."

After being enveloped in a bear hug by her namesake, Magdalina waved her goodbyes and returned to the apartment, satiated from hunger, but not from thirst.

She concocted ways of pacifying her growing bloodlust, *legally.*

Mayhap I should offer my services to the rulers of this village to rid it of any murders awaiting their turn at the executioner's block. Although, admitting to being a vampire would, in all likelihood, lead them to lopping off my *head.*

The longer she contemplated ulterior methods of hunting, the thirstier she became.

She prowled around the main room, trying to counteract the desire for blood.

The wizardry known as television was more likely to send her into a feeding frenzy than ease her agitation.

She sought solace in the journal.

It had become a source of enlightenment, especially with regards to the innovations created by ingenious minds. It was also a way to reacquaint herself with Cristoff... Chris through the lives he led.

He was a prolific diarist, his musings painting a picture as clearly as though she had experienced the events alongside him.

She had dipped into the volume here and there, but in an effort to divert her mind from its unnatural instinct, she opened it at the first page.

January 5th 1800
My name is Cristoff, but I have been known by many names. Currently I am known as Kit, a diminutive of Christopher, my family name is Prestcote, and I am the second son of an earl.

Doubtless, given the festering tensions between England and France, I will assume my commission in the army in the not too distant future.

I found this journal, tucked behind an old volume of Chaucer's works, in a wonderfully quaint bookshop on Old Compton Street, owned by a Mr Abbot. I cannot fathom what prompted me to purchase this item, save a need to document my lives.

Lives... Magdalina mulled over his choice of word. That he had chronicled this knowledge took no small amount of fortitude and, in the generation when he began the journal, could well have had him committed to an asylum, had anyone else read it.

Did he struggle with the awareness he was not living his first life, or even his fifth? How did he cope? Such awareness could cause madness. She would ask upon his return.

The next few entries were daily jottings, and of little interest, until she came to February 20th.

My parents introduced me to a delightful lady this past weekend. They have high hopes of a match.

Magdalina's chest pinched, but she continued. That he married during any one of his thirteen existences while not unexpected, did not mean she had to like it.

I cannot deny she is attractive, and am certain she possesses all the qualities expected of a prospective bride, but my heart is untouched.

Magdalina smiled a secret smile and her disquiet subsided.

She read on and, although this proposed match was mentioned again, Cristoff, or Kit in that life, held fast. Before the London Season... whatever that meant... was in full swing, he had absented himself from the city to join his regiment.

The following pages were devoted to all things military and Magdalina found echoes of their own sword training in his descriptions.

The date changed dramatically. Jumping from 1801 to 1820.

16th September 1820
Imagine my surprise when, this morning in a book shop, I felt I ought to recognize, I came across a journal on the same shelf where, I postulate, I found it the first time.

The moment I opened it, I was flooded with memories.

If given to fancy, I might attribute it to Fate. Being of more practical mind, I claim coincidence.

That said, unearthing a book, I believe I began in a past life is nothing short of preposterous, so, who am I to question the method by which we were reunited?

Magdalina grinned at his whimsy, harking back to what he said about always finding it in the same place. Books might have the power to transport the reader to other worlds, illusory or otherwise, but they were inanimate objects.

An image of the journal growing legs and marching itself back to the bookshop on Cristoff's death, popped into Magdalina's mind, making her giggle irreverently.

She turned the page, and the next and the next, wholly immersed in what Cristoff had seen and the world changing events he had witnessed.

The death of Napoleon Bonaparte, a man Cristoff labeled an egotistical menace. The opening of the first public railway in the world, from Stockton to Darlington, two towns in a land called England.

Magdalina took a break when she read this, to leaf through the book Cristoff said contained every fact anyone ever wanted to know.

The conveyance referred to as a train enthralled her. A way to travel with unheard of speed and no necessity to rest horses. What ingenuity.

Mentions of explorers and their discoveries, the invention of something described as an electric motor, and the introduction of a police service, the latter apparently set up to maintain law and order.

What happened to their guards? she pondered.

The accession of a queen to the throne of England, whose husband seemed to be a man ahead of his time.

The dates leapt forward again.

Wars — he had written a lengthy passage about the American Civil War. Magdalina curled her lip at the title. *How could a war ever be considered 'civil'? What did they do, dance away their discord?*

This made her chuckle.

Famine, social hardship. Advancements in science and medicine.

An underlined notation intrigued her. <u>*In 1878, following a war between Turkey and Russia, the Treaty of Berlin granted Romania independence.*</u>

Independence!

Glad Cristoff had included this snippet, Magdalina felt a twinge of sadness that, for a period of history, her lands had lost their autonomy.

Was the foreign rule harsh or fair? She would never know, unless Cristoff had some information in one of his books.

She added this to her internal list of things to ask him, and continued reading.

A mountain on a remote island, Krakatoa, erupted with such violence, it was heard thousands of miles away, lasted six months, and killed countless people.

Magdalina was so engrossed, she nearly missed a note at the bottom of one page.

It followed yet another jotting about the expectations of his family that he would marry and produce an heir. Cristoff, it seemed, had been fortunate to keep being reborn to wealthy or noble parents. Evidently, while this could be restrictive, it allowed him to fulfill his passion for all things ancient.

She squinted at the writing, Cristoff might have lived

several lifetimes, but his spidery penmanship did not improve.

I understand the responsibility to continue a bloodline, but I will only ever marry for love.
From the moment I failed my beloved Magdalina, I have not found a woman equal to her in beauty, wit and intelligence, despite her being a virago when riled.
My heart remains hers and will do so forever.

Magdalina traced the words, her heart thudded and warmth suffused her.

The pang of jealousy sparked by the realization Cristoff probably loved and bedded women throughout the last thousand years, and sharpened by the damn dragon, continued to lurk on the periphery of her mind — even though it was clear, Elena was no threat.

Never were so few words imbued with so much power.

Concentrating, she imagined her envy and mistrust to be a ball hovering above her hand. With a swift flick of her wrist she, figuratively, expelled the malignant emotions, effectively eradicating them.

"I refuse to let you cause a rift between Cristoff and me," she spoke quietly but her voice rang with authority. "I might have to cater to this craving for blood, but it will be on my terms. Not yours."

Confident she had made her point… and ignoring the fact that demons probably did not take kindly to being ordered about by puny humans, even if she *was* a vampire… Magdalina poured herself a glass of wine from the open bottle on the kitchen counter.

The full-bodied red slid over her throat like a caress. Not quite blood, but a fair substitute.

Quelling the urge to hunt for a victim, Magdalina resumed her seat and buried herself in Cristoff's writings.

Shipwrecks, the invention of what looked like a mechanical bird — her stomach roiled at the description — it sounded frightening and ridiculously dangerous.

More war. This time, *The Great War*, a term which made no real sense, dragging in half the world and resulting in immeasurable losses for, as far as she could tell, very little gain.

Nothing particularly great about it, in her opinion.

On and on she read, occasionally returning to his eloquent declaration. His script might lack finesse, but his rendering was pure poetry.

She came to the last pages, the ones she had seen on her first night in this apartment.

She had reached his twelfth life.

A curious melancholy stole over her.

Yes, he had found her, but would it all be in vain? His diligence, his painstaking efforts, dying, being reborn; searching always searching, and through it all his fealty to her never wavered. He must be exhausted.

She wanted him to come home, she wanted to tell him she appreciated his dedication, steadfast devotion and… did she have the courage to articulate it?… his unshakeable love.

A more urgent demand required her attention. Whether she liked it or not, she needed to feed.

Only once, had she ventured out after nightfall cloaked the township. She preferred Cristoff not see her voracious thirst, or how she quenched it.

She looked out of the window, the moon was high, bathing the buildings in a celestial glow, transforming what the inhabitants took for granted into something out of a fairy tale.

She was thankful fairy tales were awash with unscrupulous individuals. These were the ones she sought. Their essence might be less palatable than people of Ms. Radu's ilk but, if she prevented even one villain from hurting an innocent, her conscience was clear.

Melding with the shadows, Magdalina slipped along gloomy alleys towards the disreputable neighborhoods, her acute sense of smell homing in on prospective targets. One or two she noted as possibilities, but carried on. She had learnt to distinguish the perfect prey.

She soon found it.

Rounding a corner, she came upon a man venting his fury on a skinny dog, who whimpered piteously as it tried to avoid the stick.

Enraged at the man's brutality, Magdalina crept up behind him.

"Why sir, to beat a defenseless creature says little for your rectitude. What harm could this poor mongrel have done to warrant so egregious a bout of temper?" her tone, hypnotic.

He spun around, snarling, "What business is it of y—" he stopped, the power of speech deserting him when his gaze fell on the goddess of a woman who had the temerity to question his behavior.

The stick dropped from nerveless fingers, hitting the ground with a muted thunk.

The dog cowered against a wall, its huge eyes watchful.

"I dislike cruelty of any form, so I shall make this as painless as possible."

Her fangs pierced the soft flesh of his neck before he could utter a squawk of protest. His eyes rolled back and his body folded in on itself as she drained him with consummate expertise.

Breathing heavily, she let him fall to the damp street, and wiped her mouth with one of Cristoff's enormous handkerchiefs, tucked into one of her pockets for this exact purpose.

The haze of bloodlust dissipated.

The dog did not move.

"Hello, my precious." she crouched down and held out a hand which trembled slightly.

From a safe distance, the dog sniffed her outstretched fingers, and risked a lick; its tongue, gentle.

"He cannot hurt you anymore," she said. "Go, be free."

Standing, Magdalina felt the restorative energy of the man's life force seeping through her body, strengthening it. She began the long trek back to the apartment.

She had barely taken ten steps when a soft padding sound made her glance down. The scrawny creature was walking next to her, its tail up, ears pricked, and eyes gleaming.

"Shoo." She flapped her hands. "I cannot care for you."

The dog canted its head and gave her what she surmised to be the doggy equivalent of a grin.

She groaned. *Now what what am I supposed to do?* Hoping the dog would get bored and run off to find his canine friends, she continued on her way.

The dog never left her side.

Cursing her irresponsible actions from now to the end of time, Magdalina acknowledged, had she not intervened, the dog would have died. Something she could not, in good conscience, have allowed, but it left her with a bigger problem.

Chris might not like dogs, although Cristoff always had hounds. His apartment was not suited to an animal. The people who owned the building might not permit any kind of creature.

She was still mulling over what to do when she reached Elena's Bistro.

Vasili was sitting outside, smoking a malodorous pipe. He inclined his head in a tacit greeting when he saw Magdalina, his eyes widening when he spotted the dog.

"You know there is a dog following you?" he rumbled in amusement.

"Yes," Magdalina sighed. "I cannot understand his affection. All I did was save him from a beating."

Vasili gaped. "Beg pardon?"

She repeated her remark, adding, "Well I couldn't allow the man to kill the poor thing. That would not do."

"You are unhurt?" Vasili got to his feet and came closer, running a practiced eye over the woman.

"I am… okay." She recalled Chris's favorite word. "He did me no harm, but now I have a conundrum."

"What to do with your canine companion." Vasili finished for her. He studied the dog who dropped to its haunches and stared back.

"Male or female?" Vasili asked.

Magdalina shrugged. "I did not stop to check."

Minutes later, after establishing the dog was female and would benefit from a decent meal and a bath, Vasili — his compassion at odds with his bluff appearance — said he would take the creature.

"Magda had been pestering me to buy her a dog for months. This way, I don't need to pay, and I get a guard dog into the bargain."

Dubious as to how good a guard dog the creature would be, Magdalina was eternally grateful to Vasili for his generous offer.

"Thank you, Vasili, I appreciate your gesture. I know you will give her the loving home she deserves."

"Aye, well," he replied gruffly. "That's as may be. Are you sure you are not hurt?"

"I am fine." Magdalina smiled and took her leave, patting the dog's scruffy head.

"You be good, now," she instructed and hurried back to the apartment.

Chapter Twelve

A sustained pounding stirred Magdalina from a sound slumber. For a split-second, she was transported back to the sarcophagus and the boom of cannon fire.

The ceaseless knocking did not abate, and she peeled back languid lids. On the verge of haranguing whoever dared disturb her rest, recollection slammed into her and she lurched off the couch in a panic.

Scurrying to the door, she pressed her ear against the wood. It could not be Cristoff. He was not due back for several days.

It must be the City Guard, or the Politia, or whatever their current title was, Magdalina's sleep-addled brain hazarded, exacerbating her alarm.

You have been so careless when disposing of your victims. You will be brought to justice for your crimes.

I do not even think the dragon can save—

"Magdalina are you there? If you are, please open the door," a familiar female voice beseeched from the other side, "I am about to drop everything out here."

Sagging with relief, Magdalina had barely unlatched the

door, when Elena burst through, her arms laden with packages, and a container, Magdalina deduced to be coffee by its heavenly scent.

Elena made a beeline for the table, Cristoff had declared a work-free food zone…

People nowadays attribute the strangest names to their furniture.

…and began to set up a spread which, in Magdalina's opinion, could feed a small army.

"Good morning, lazy-bones," Elena chirped cheerfully. "Doctor Chris rang to ask me to let you know he will be home tonight. Why he did not call you direct, I am not sure."

She arched a brow at the dazed-looking woman who was trying to understand what prompted Elena's early morning visit.

Elena dismissed her own question with a toss of her head, her chestnut brown curls tumbling around her shoulders.

"Okay, get over here and make yourself comfortable before my delicious food gets cold; a travesty I cannot abide."

"You did not need to bother yourself—"

Elena interjected, "That man interrupted my morning schedule, begging me to deliver a message. Did he expect me to arrive empty handed?"

Feigning exasperation, Elena ran her fingers through her hair to straighten it. "Men know nothing of social etiquette, make sure you teach him properly."

It was apparent to Magdalina, that although Elena knew and maintained an amicable demeanor with all her patrons, she had, possibly for some time, lacked something most women took for granted — a friend.

Elena poured two cups of coffee, and held one out to Magdalina. "Shall we?"

Magdalina wrapped her fingers around the warm cup and inhaled. The robust aroma clearing the last of her drowsiness. "Am I costing you more *allowance*?" parroting Magda's word.

"Hardly, I have Vasili and Magda tending to the morning rush. She enjoys bossing her papa around. A natural merchant, that girl.

Elena paused long enough to sip her coffee, "Oh, and next time you allow a stray to follow you home, make sure it is a cute, bearded hunk, not some furry critter, in which case, come to me. Vasili might not appreciate the competition." Her grin, nothing short of roguish.

"I am deeply sorry," Magdalina apologized, not entirely sure she understood Elena's inference, but unwilling to look foolish. "I had not the heart to chase the poor creature away after what it had suffered. I had no mind to instigate a dilemma."

While Elena did not appear to be vexed, Magdalina was out of practice at reading subtle nuances, particularly those exploited with devastating effect by women.

She took refuge in her coffee. As the brew touched her lips, Magdalina understood why most could not handle her friend's drink. It was like liquid fire, but a welcome substitute for blood.

Elena waved her hand, acknowledging and dismissing Magdalina's concerns in the simple gesture. "Care to guess what my lamb named that scruffy mutt? Doctor Chris. I cannot imagine what the poor man will think when he learns a female dog has been named after him."

Magdalina snorted into the steamy brew. "Excuse me?" She lowered her cup, interested to hear the story behind this decision.

"Yes, Magda decided to name the mongrel after our friend. I tried to explain that the creature ought to have a girl's name, but my daughter can be very stubborn when the mood takes her, arguing girls are often named Chris.

"Once she gets started, there is no stopping her. I have no idea where she gets that from."

"If this mountain of food is any example, I would surmise, her mother."

They shared a conspiratorial grin.

Elena assessed the orderly chaos of the room as she bit into one of her crepes. "How does someone so meticulous in his day-to-day work, live in such disarray? Ought we to tidy it up for the good doctor, a kind of welcome home gift?"

"I would be afraid to misplace something important," Magdalina demurred.

"You know what's what..." Elena refused to be dissuaded. "...so you deal with that, and the dusting, and I'll tackle the vacuuming."

"Dusting? Vacuuming?" Magdalina could not mask her confusion.

"Dusting, surely you have dusted?" She studied Magdalina, forehead creased.

Whether they were in the twelfth century or the twentieth, cleaning would never constitute part of Magdalina's duties. That chore was relegated to servants. Probably not an excuse Elena would believe.

"Cleaning the surfaces with a cloth... and, vacuuming," Elena mimed the action. "We may have just rid ourselves of President Ceaușescu and his wife, but that does not mean we are living in the dark ages. "

You have no idea what that was like, Magdalina mused inwardly. *I must ask Cristoff about all these modern terms. I do not want people questioning my blunders.*

Outwardly she gave an apologetic smile. "Ahhh, dusting yes. That came under what my mai... mother," she amended quickly, "referred to as domestic chores."

The meal finished, the pair set about putting the apartment to rights. When Magdalina came to Cristoff's paperwork, she did no more than arrange it into neat piles, easily retrievable when required.

Prudently, she concealed his journal behind a number of books on the middle shelf of the bookcase. Her inability to explain the peculiarities of her vampiric existence to her new friend, would be magnified if Elena learned their mutual friend had lived at least thirteen lives. No sense sending the woman to an early grave.

It was then she noticed a dusty scroll, bound, and seemingly discarded at the back of the same shelf.

About to reach for it, an ear-splitting noise emanating from the weapon Elena was using on a tapestry — which, to Magdalina's mystification, was displayed on the floor instead of hanging on one of the walls — gave her a start. She jerked her arm out of the gap, knocking some trinkets off a table.

Grumbling at her clumsiness, she picked them up, all but forgetting the scroll, which Cristoff must have designated as unimportant.

Concerned Elena might lose control of whatever she was using to grapple with the artwork, Magdalina escaped into Cristoff's bedroom. The one room she had not dared to enter.

Sitting on his bed, she could sense him with every breath, and yearned for his return. They had skirted around their seething emotions long enough. It was time to face the truth.

The cacophony from the other room stopped abruptly, to be replaced by Elena's far more melodious tones "Magdalina, where did you get to?"

Magdalina slipped out of the bedroom and along the hall

into the main living area. "Did you defeat the tapestry?" she prevaricated.

"What? No... whatever... no, you have to see this."

On the magic picture box, a man was describing a grisly discovery.

Bucharest Politia were notified by a local resident who had discovered the man's body in an alley on the perimeter of the housing projects. While officials will neither confirm nor deny the state of the deceased, an anonymous source has reported the corpse was entirely drained of blood.

The mayor's office has issued a warning to all residents to take extra precautions when they traverse the city at night.

In other news....

Elena turned off the television. Her expression, one of amazement. "Incredible is it not?"

"What do you mean?" Magdalina asked. "That is a terrible way to die."

"I agree, but given the history of this city, it would be no coincidence if someone was killed in that manner."

"I do not understand."

"Bucharest was founded by the greatest vampire who ever lived. Vlad the Impaler or, as he was also known..." Elena paused theatrically, "...Dracula, well, according to Bram Stoker."

Her Romanian accent emphasized her mock menacing tone, and she parodied a pair of fangs with her index fingers.

"I want to suck your blood, giiiiirrrrl." She leered comically

While the amusement value was lost on Magdalina — who had never heard of Bram Stoker — circumstances as they were, she summoned up an obligatory and genuine-sounding chuckle.

"You are humorous, Elena."

Elena glanced at her watch. "Wow, is that the time? I have to get back, or you two will have nothing to eat tonight."

"Shall we be dining at your bistro, or will Chris get it as…" she wracked her brain for the phrase he used "…takeaway?"

"Oh, with us definitely. We want to hear all about Doctor Chris's trip."

Magdalina looked down at her rumpled attire. She had no clothes, save the outfit and set of scrubs she had stolen from the intern, reduced to alternating between them and a pair of Cristoff's pj's, which were, apparently, sleep attire.

Assuming Magdalina had lost her suitcase somewhere on her travels, Elena took pity on her. "Just along the street there's a seamstress. Her name is Ioana. She is a bitter hag, but tell her I sent you anyway. She owes me a favor."

She collected her crockery and headed out, caroling playfully, "Do not let the son of the dragon get you."

Magdalina closed the door and leaned against it, her mind churning.

Does Elena believe in vampires? If so, maybe she knows the name of the one who cursed me?

She demanded in stentorian tones, "Dragon, come to me. I know your name. Vlad Țepeș. I command you to free me."

Scornful mirth filled her brain.

"You are witless if you believe that sot to be me. I offered his father the same arrangement, I afforded your ancestor, Decebalus, in order to liberate your lands of invaders. The foolish son saw it as a blank invitation to squander precious blood.

"A great leader. A vampire. *Bah*," the Dragon snarled his irritation.

"He was nothing more than a crazed killer. Can you

imagine being one of his nobles, ordered to dine in a field among thousands of decaying, impaled corpses? Your master of ceremonies, Vlad, sitting in the midst of the carnage, munching away happily, threatening to skewer anyone who refused.

"Even I have my limits for senseless destruction. In the end, he paid his debt by having his head offered to the Sultan of the Ottoman Empire as an ornament to be hung above his city gate.

"Now, hush and do not bother me again, until *I* summon you."

Chapter Thirteen

Magdalina sank onto the sofa, chewing her lip. Buying clothes. Something she had never done, did not even know how. *The seamstress must be gifted indeed if she can make a gown in less than a day.*

It came to her that she would like to impress Cristoff. The apparel she had worn since her unceremonious advent into this peculiar age was shapeless, the footwear uncomfortable. A trickle of excitement ran down her spine at the notion of a new gown.

Wait… womenfolk in this town did not wear gowns, at least, not what she would refer to as a gown. Many wore garb similar to that of her maids, although indecorously short, revealing an indecent amount of leg.

Some dressed like the men whose tunics were more fitted and shorter than in her day, while their stockings appeared quite loose.

That said, the effect was one of comfortable practicality, and quite liberating, she imagined.

"Oh, to feel pretty again," she said, dreamily, to the empty room.

With Magdalina, to think was to act. Making sure she looked respectable, and muttering a grudging thanks to Elena for chivvying her into cleaning the apartment, Magdalina pocketed the wad of notes, locked the door, and set out.

She strolled along the street, riveted by the hustle and bustle, biting her lip, so as not to shriek at the sight of the metal wagons, Cristoff had informed her were cars, hurtling along the road. They were so loud.

Was the train, she had read about, equally noisy? Magdalina shuddered, revising her opinion on *that* mode of travel. How the populace endured the constant barrage to their ears, baffled her.

Mindful of the speeding objects, Magdalina was determined not to be intimidated, while she inspected the shop windows. Like Elena's Bistro, most advertised their wares in their signage, and those which flummoxed her, she avoided.

Magdalina came to a window emblazoned with the words *Ioana's House of Fashion*.

She peered through the glass. Around the interior several women posed, clad in a variety of raiment. She pushed open the door, the jangle of the bell announcing her entrance, surprised when none of the ladies moved.

Magdalina dithered uncertainly. About to turn on her heel, her flight was stayed by an impatient voice which spoke from somewhere beyond the frozen females.

"I'm coming, I'm coming." The sound of shuffling, then a wizened crone seemed to manifest right in front of her, an abundance of material in her arms.

She resembled some of the drawings in one of Cristoff's volumes about folklore, so closely that Magdalina had to stifle a startled squeak.

"May I help you?" the woman straightened up, and Magdalina realized she was not as old as she first appeared.

Perhaps she was afflicted by a bone disorder. Something Magdalina had seen many times among the peasants. Paucity of sufficient food, the usual cause.

"I should be pleased to purchase some clothes, if you would be so kind," Magdalina said, hoping this was the correct way to broach the subject. She frowned. The other women had yet to acknowledge her presence, they remained like statues.

"Elena sent me," she added, presuming this to be the Ioana of the sign and Elena's recommendation.

"Pah," Ioana spat. "Elena, she praises my skill, and buys off the peg." Shaking her head in resignation. "Still, she often sends me boxes of cakes to serve to my customers, so…"

The woman made a curious gesture as though weighing things in her palms, which Magdalina took to mean the treats balanced out Elena's choice of clothing, while wondering what on earth *off the peg* signified.

"What do you require?" The woman appraised Magdalina, measuring her up without making a single jotting.

Magdalina opened her hands, helplessly. "I am at a loss. Something I am able to wear during the day, and something for being escorted to a dining establishment."

If Ioana was taken aback by Magdalina's archaic way of speaking, she gave no sign. Merely tapped her foot, and studied her client.

"I have it." She whisked around the room, and to Magdalina's dismay, divested three of the other women of their clothing with a swift flick of her wrist.

"Here, try these."

Before Magdalina could apologize to the poor customers who still, to her consternation, had not moved, Ioana ushered her through a curtain into a spacious room, in the middle of which stood a square box, and two more customers.

Around the walls, smaller cubicles each with a floor to ceiling reflecting glass.

Unable to curb her curiosity about the motionless females, Magdalina approached one of them in the guise of checking out the outfit.

Biting down on a sheepish giggle, she was inordinately relieved to discover they were not human at all but rather crude sculptures.

She stored that away to tell Cristoff later, suspecting he would be amused by her mistake.

"Any one… they're all empty. Quiet at this time of day," Ioana encouraged.

Magdalina could not decide whether she was being praised or chastised for disrupting Ioana's morning. Preferring to think it was the former, she ventured into one of the cubicles.

Ioana followed and the garments, now draped on a piece of wood with a metal hook poking out of the middle, were hung in a line on a long thin bar of metal.

"This era is exhausting," Magdalina muttered under her breath. "What happened to the dressmaker coming to your abode? That was so much easier."

She had become proficient at removing Ms. Radu's attire, but the new outfits looked a trifle more complicated. She studied them, shrugged, and hoped for the best.

The skirt was easy, and fitted perfectly, the slightly flared style suited her height, and the color… a deep, midnight blue… complemented her ebony hair and ivory skin.

The bodice — a silky material in a pastel hue, which reminded Magdalina of the lake near the fortress when it froze — slipped over her head and had no buttons. Not dissimilar to the man's tunic, it sat neatly on her waistline rather than falling to her knees.

She stared at her reflection. If not for her raven tresses and apprehensive blue eyes, she was unrecognizable.

"Let me see," Ioana bade.

Gingerly, afraid she might rip the delicate material, Magdalina walked out of the cubicle, to be met by Ioana's critical eye.

"Not bad, not bad. Maybe..." she hurried out, returning seconds later with two more items... and so it began. A morning of trying on, being inspected, trying on something else.

Ioana might be, erroneously, considered an old crone, but she was an artist, and not satisfied unless she judged an outfit perfect.

It also became clear — as the seamstress regaled Magdalina with hilarious tales about growing up in the neighborhood — that the relationship between Elena and Ioana was like squabbling siblings.

Her head swimming with the different clothes, shoes, and accessories, she had been persuaded into, Magdalina stood at the counter watching Ioana wrap each item in tissue paper and slide it into a large bag.

The tranquility of the shop was shattered when the door was flung open with such force, it almost flew off its hinges.

Silhouetted in the frame, a tall imperious-looking woman. Dressed like something from one of the television shows Magdalina found jarring, the newcomer's face was all but hidden behind an enormous pair of dark spectacles. Cristoff referred to them as sunglasses, worn to shield the wearer's eyes from the sun's glare.

"My couture," she demanded haughtily, without greeting Ioana.

"A moment, Madame, I am..."

"A moment? Goodness, Ioana, I do not pay your exorbitant prices to *have a moment*. I am terribly busy and Jacques is waiting for me in the car."

She slid the sunglasses down her nose to peer over them, dismissing Magdalina with a supercilious glance.

"I am sure your... this... person does not mind waiting." her tone indicating Magdalina possessed less importance than a cockroach.

Embarrassed, Ioana's cheeks flushed with hectic color. She began to point out that Magdalina was in the middle of settling her account, when the latter interposed smoothly.

"Do not fret, Ioana. I am not in a hurry. Evidently, this... lady's need is greater than mine and, in her desire to collect her beautiful clothes, painstakingly made by you, forgot to bring her manners."

The woman glared down her patrician nose, trying to determine whether she had been insulted, but blessed with little intelligence was unable to decide. She opted to ignore the remark, and all but shooed Ioana into the rear of the shop.

With an apologetic gesture to Magdalina, Ioana dealt with the newcomer, who threw her money on the counter disdainfully and stalked out, ordering the hapless Jacques to relieve her of her purchases and stow them in the car.

The huge vehicle roared off leaving the two in the shop lost for words.

"Forgive her intrusion," Ioana said with a moue of distaste. "Odeta... sorry," she adopted a patronizing tone, "Madame Barreau believes herself very influential. She married a wealthy Frenchman and likes to lord it over the rest of us. To think she used to be a whore." Ioana shook her head.

Magdalina, resenting the woman's attitude, had taken pains to read the entry in Ioana's account book, committing Madame Barreau's address to memory. It cost nothing to be respectful, especially to the women who had no doubt worked her fingers to the bone to produce the superb garments.

The behaviour of Madame *I am better than you* Barreau would not go unpunished.

Assuring Ioana she had nothing to apologize for, Magdalina paid her bill, which had been heavily discounted, thanked the seamstress effusively, and affirmed she would return, if only to hear more stories about Ioana's life, and the changes wrought on her country.

Chapter Fourteen

Her purchases unpacked and hung neatly in what she assumed to be the modern equivalent of a clothes chest, and eminently more practical, Magdalina poured herself a glass of wine and made herself comfortable at the large table.

Unaware of what time Cristoff would be home, she flicked through the pile of source material he had collated.

As happened every time she studied them, Magdalina was astounded by his diligence and sheer unerring perseverance. Most people would have given up at the first hurdle. As far as he knew, she was dead, buried in an unmarked grave, and lost to history. That delectable warmth coiled around her and she could not prevent the silly smile which twitched at her lips.

"You are like a dizzy damsel, Magdalina," she chided herself. "Not a jaded queen." She chuckled and, squashing her girlish nonsense, concentrated on the documents.

An hour ticked by, and she was no closer to an answer than the first time she picked up a manuscript. In a fit of pique, and suppressing the inclination to indulge in a temper tantrum, she shoved the stack near her elbow, which… inevitably… toppled off the desk. Papers floated in random directions, coming to land in disordered heaps on the tapestry.

"Well, is that not just the feather to my arrow." She glared at the mess. Muttering her vexation, Magdalina dropped onto her knees to gather them into the correct order. One caught her eye. She sank back on her heels to scrutinize it.

Not a single sheet, this was several, bound at the left-hand side by a fraying ribbon, which she doubted was the original binding. Quickly affirmed when it became apparent, this document could be dated to within fifty years of her reign.

"No way," Magdalina imitated a character from one of the television shows, she watched.

Standing, the rest of the invaluable codices slithering, forgotten, off her lap, she resumed her seat at the table. Picking up one of Cristoff's pens, and opening the notebook they were sharing, she jotted down her findings.

The trickle of words became a cascade, pages covered with her scribble, as she translated the ancient text.

How did we miss this? she asked herself. *It changes everything.*

Only when she had to squint at the paper did she register the afternoon was waning. She leaned back in the chair, the muscles in her neck and her shoulders groaning their disapproval at being in the same position for hours.

She switched on the light, and glanced at the apparatus on the wall, Cristoff had dubbed a clock. That was no help. Going to the window, she surmised, taking into account the time of year and that the sun was almost at the horizon, it was around Vespers.

Knowing the precise hour had never been an essential part of her life; her routine governed by the daylight. She rose shortly after dawn, ate when she was hungry, and, if not entertaining visitors, retired at dusk.

Time, in this century, dictated everything. It was hard to accept its constraints, made worse given she did not understand how it was apportioned across the day and night.

Naught she could do about it now, but she wanted to be ready when Chris came home, so she closed the book and left the sheaf alongside.

Reveling in a long hot shower, an invention of which she approved highly — made even better now she was acquainted with the mechanics of taps — Magdalina thought about the looming reunion. She was excited and nervous, and not only because of her recent discovery.

Dry and wrapped in a towel, she padded to her bedroom and opened the cupboard. Gentle fingers stroked over the new clothes, the material whispering in the stillness.

She lifted out the hanger sporting a pair of charcoal gray trousers — the modern equivalent of hose — and a three-quarter sleeved relaxed-fit blouse in a color Ioana had described as soft peach.

Trousers, so Ioana assured, were no longer worn exclusively by men. Occasionally, Magdalina had risked the wrath of the males in her private household by flouting convention and wearing hose when she rode, or during sword training, but never at court.

The freedom of movement this garment afforded could not be underestimated, and she had been coaxed into two pairs by the canny seamstress. Hopefully, Cristoff would not be upset by her choice.

She was studying her reflection when she heard the click of the lock and the soft chafing of the door across the polished wooden floor. Her heart hiccupped. They parted on less than congenial terms, would his return be similarly tense?

Magdalina had replayed that last scene over and over in her head, acknowledging her behavior bordered on that of a precocious princess not a well-bred queen.

The long, lonely hours had given her plenty of time to ponder her belligerence, conceding Cristoff's comment had not been intended to hurt, more a gentle taunt. She blamed her over-reaction, a rare occurrence, on the welter of contrary emotions she was battling.

What if she confessed her affection?

To outward appearances Cristoff reciprocated her feelings, but they were different people now. No longer queen and liegeman. No longer secret lovers. She was an undead vampire. He kept being reborn. Both enduring an immortality of sorts.

Could they breach the divide?

"Magdalina?" Cristoff's voice bore a hint of concern.

She went, with some hesitancy, into the main room.

His imposing figure never failed to take her breath away, but this evening, she seemed to lose all ability to function.

She opened her mouth to speak, nothing came out.

Cristoff stared, his eyes wide as he beheld her metamorphosis. Still a queen…she would always be a queen…she had gained something more, like an inner radiance. He could not quite put his finger on it, except that it was enchanting.

"You look… I like… how did…" he stammered incoherently.

"Ioana," Magdalina said, as though that explained everything.

Cristoff nodded absently. "Utterly bewitching," he murmured.

"Cristoff." Magdalina coerced her brain. "Please forgive my outburst. It was petulant and discourteous after your unqualified kindness." She eyed him warily.

"You have nothing to apologize for. I spoke—"

"You spoke with honesty, and I threw it back in your face."

"Water under the bridge." Cristoff grinned suddenly.

Although this was yet another incomprehensible phrase, Magdalina did not bother to question it, taking a guess at the gist.

"I missed you," she admitted shyly.

"I missed you too, and have been dreaming of doing this since I left."

He closed the gap and, before she could protest... if that was at all likely... she was in his arms being kissed with an ardor which left her weak at the knees.

"C-Cristoff," she gasped when they finally came up for air, "does this mean... or am I being... would you...?" she trailed off, unable to broach the one question, his reply to which she feared.

"Yes. No. Yes," Cristoff replied with a wicked smile.

"Oh you..." she elbowed him in the stomach. "Might I be so bold as to ask whether the words you wrote are how you feel... truly feel?"

"And which words might those be?" Cristoff's green eyes glinted with amusement.

Bracing herself, she quoted, "I understand the responsibility to continue a bloodline, but I will only ever marry for love. From the moment I failed my beloved Magdalina, I have not found a woman equal to her in beauty, wit and intelligence, despite her being a virago when riled. My heart remains hers and will do so forever."

"Ahh, so you have been reading my journal," he evaded a direct answer. "I trust you found it... illuminating."

An unaccustomed twinge speared Magdalina's heart and she felt the color ebb from her cheeks.

"Never mind. More water under your bridge," she trilled

airily, unable to mask the tremor in her voice. Obviously his fantasy did not match this new reality.

Pinning a bright smile on her face, she turned. Before she had taken a single step, his arm tightened around her, and she was pulled flush against his burly frame.

"Where do you think you're going?" he growled in her ear.

"I th-thought perhaps since… you know…" she floundered.

"What, that now I have found you, after all these centuries, you no longer drive me to distraction?"

"Well…" she mourned, "I am not quite the same, am I, after withering in a coffin for eons. Not exactly the stuff of romance, is it?"

"Okay, so maybe our romance is unorthodox. When did you ever abide by the rules?"

Magdalina chuckled. "Fair enough." She caressed his face, fingernails scratching the fine stubble hugging his jaw, as she felt herself drowning in the viridian depths of his eyes. All her misgivings fell away.

"I love you, Cristoff. I will love you until the stars fall out of the sky."

The divide was breached with intoxicating effectiveness, and neither spoke for a *very* long time.

When the world realigned itself, Magdalina remembered her discovery.

"Oh, before I forget, I was going through the papers again when I came across something which affects us both in ways you could never suspect."

Chapter Fifteen

C ristoff ran his mind back over the pile of evidence they had read, seemingly, back to front, inside out, and upside down. "What did we miss?"

"It was a sheaf, to which neither of us accorded credence because there was no mention of dragons or demons or curses. "

"How, then, does it pertain to our search?"

"It alters the framework. Come." She took his hand and, leading him to the table, pointed to the fragile sheets of parchment. "Sit, sit," she instructed.

Cristoff swallowed a grin and did as she asked.

"Firstly, and something I paid no attention to before, this is high quality vellum, indicating it is a document of significance. Secondly, lack of salient detail rendered it an outlier, and worthless to your investigation. I am surprised it remained in your collection, but I am glad you did not destroy it."

"I would never destroy an artifact," Cristoff was scandalized.

"Fine, hand it over to one of your museum places. Don't

interrupt," she scolded, to his amusement. "Neither of us divined its value and had set it aside. This afternoon, I was perusing the collection again, hoping to unlock the key to this aggravating mystery when I..." she flushed, "...err... became a tad... hmmm... irritated."

"You chucked a hissy fit." Knowing her extremely well, Cristoff's amusement blossomed into outright mirth.

"I did *what?*"

Laughing, Cristoff clarified, sneaking a kiss as he did.

"I suppose," she agreed diffidently, the heat in her cheeks, no longer anything to do with embarrassment. "Anyway..." using another of this modern Chris's favorite terms, "...as I was picking up the papers, I spotted this one and a couple of words caught my eye. Family names. My family's names."

"*Your* family?"

Magdalina nodded. "Presumably, this is why you identified it as important initially, but without mention of the dragon, ignored it. It intrigued me enough that I translated the whole thing. Essentially, it is our bloodline."

"Your bloodline," he corrected.

"No, Cristoff... ours." She sat back, beaming exultantly.

"Wait, we are related?" Cristoff's expression morphed from interested to appalled.

"Yes but, before you start to panic, not closely. I think you are a distant cousin. Do you think I would declare my undying devotion if I thought we were brother and sister, or immediate cousins, illegitimate or otherwise? Give me some credit," she tutted.

"Thank goodness for that." Cristoff pulled a comical face and blew a relieved sigh. "Okay, spill."

"Spill what?" Perplexed, Magdalina twisted in her chair to stare around them, her nose crinkling.

"Oh, my love." He drew her as close as their seated positions allowed. "Don't hit me, but your bemusement is so adorable I can't help but toss out words, just to watch your face. It means please tell me."

He scattered butterfly soft kisses across her throat and neck, in delicious digression.

Magdalina felt she ought to be annoyed but it took too much effort, so she made do with a tolerant shake of her head. "If you stop distracting me, I might consider it…" she said loftily.

Cristoff sobered, more or less. "I'm listening, sweetheart."

"Several generations before I was born, the heir and only child, a son named Florin, was killed, leaving no direct successor.

"The next in line was a cousin, Grigore, who had married a foreign noblewoman, I think her name was Zehra, the text is degraded. They are the ones through whom I am descended."

She looked at Cristoff. "With me so far?"

His response, an eloquently quirked brow.

"Just checking." Magdalina chuckled.

"According to this text, my great, great grandfather had an illicit," she paused delicately, "liaison with someone in the court, who gave birth to a son. I suspect it was a maidservant, because although she is not named, he accepted the boy."

She pointed to a portion of the text on the second page.

"Summarizing, it says, 'His features mimic my own and I cannot deny I bedded the wench. I wanted to marry her, but my parents were adamant our bloodline not be sullied.'

"Then here…" two lines further on, "… 'I acquiesced on the proviso she remained at court under my protection, and my son and his descendants, in perpetuity, were granted noble status.'

"His parents must have agreed because, from what I can fathom, the line continued unbroken until the year I was born. I had no idea this existed, and was added to during subsequent reigns, attested by the differing penmanship. I do, however, know why it was kept a secret."

"And that would be?" Despite his sharp wit, Cristoff had not put two and two together.

"Because you are descended from my great, great grandfather and the maid."

If Magdalina had slapped him with a wet fish, Cristoff would have been less shocked.

"I'm sorry, what?" He gawked at her.

"You are the legitimate... well, true heir to the Dragoš throne.

He shook his head trying to dispel the buzzing her statement had triggered. "I'm sorry what?" he repeated.

"While we are both descended from my... our... great, great grandfather, my claim to the title queen takes second place to yours. Although your ancestor was born on the wrong side of the bed, your heritage is linked directly to his father, whereas mine was rather more circuitous.

"I was pronounced queen because, to all intents and purposes, I was the only blood relative left on the paternal side. It seems my chancellor, and his predecessors, preferred my convoluted heritage over the true lineage."

Magdalina studied Cristoff's face. "You were the rightful heir, not me. Had you been king, it is doubtful the uprising would have gained any traction. They did not like being ruled by a woman."

Cristoff did not reply immediately, dumbfounded by Magdalina's revelation. *I should have been king. Well, that was a pretty pickle.*

A matter for another time, right now, a more crucial matter required addressing. "Does that eliminate the curse?"

"I wish, but no, it makes no difference. I am still of Dragoš blood, and I broke the covenant.

"A corrupt covenant," Cristoff growled.

Magdalina shrugged. "Maybe so, but a covenant all the same. Friend Dragon would not be persecuting me, if you were his quarry."

"What's our next move?" he ruminated, out loud.

"We go to Elena's for dinner."

Magdalina's change of subject did little to staunch the tumult in Cristoff's head.

"***Dinner***?"

"Of course, Elena has been preparing something special for your homecoming." Unrepentantly, Magdalina shooed him off to the bathroom.

"Dammit, just when there was a far more interesting meal to be enjoyed." His smile, nothing short of salacious.

Magdalina burst out laughing, the tension in the room evaporating. "Go on, you reprobate. Plenty of time for that later."

Dinner at Elena's was uproarious, especially when little Magda introduced Doctor Chris Williamson — eminent archaeologist, to Doctor Chris — street accident.

To the gratitude of Elena and Magdalina, Cristoff took the meeting seriously, even shaking Doctor Chris's proffered paw, to Magda's squealed delight. He *did* make a mental note to quiz Magdalina about it in the privacy of his apartment, reading more into the appearance of a canine companion than a chance encounter.

Magdalina's new outfit was greeted with beams of approval, and the odd appreciative glance from one or two of the male customers.

Cristoff experienced an unaccustomed stab of jealousy, deliberating whether, despite Magdalina's lack of official identification, or plausible excuse for not having any, he could feasibly marry her out of hand, and whisk her away from such undisguised admiration.

Get a grip, man, he instructed himself, and managed to behave with his usual bonhomie.

So full — Magdalina had declared Chris might need to roll her home, and promising to return as soon as they had some free time to play with Magda and Doctor Chris — the two said their goodbyes and meandered back to the apartment. Cristoff entwined his fingers with Magdalina's, pleased when she responded with a gentle squeeze.

Cloaked by the cool autumnal night, they did not speak. They had no need to, content just being together.

Inside, the lights dimmed, the words both had been afraid to profess flew off trembling lips as fast as clothes flew off trembling bodies.

The centuries fell away as two people, wrenched apart by war and hate, surrendered to each other with a love unassailable.

Cristoff's seduction continued for several days... to be fair, they had a thousand years to catch up on... the couple only leaving the apartment for an occasional stroll or a meal at Elena's.

Fleetingly, everything else faded into the background.

The dragon could wait.

Chapter Sixteen

Magdalina stirred. The pale gleam of the moonbeams spilling through the uncurtained window, bathed Cristoff in an unearthly glow. Magdalina shivered, the chill of premonition creeping down her spine.

She would not let him die, not for her, not again.

Restless, and unwilling to disturb his slumber, she eased out of bed and padded through the silent apartment to the kitchen. She poured a glass of wine from the bottle they had not finished earlier, and sipped it as she wandered around the darkened living-room... a term, Magdalina still found amusing, even after Cristoff had explained why it was named thus.

She put the glass on the table, the soft chink overly-loud in the stillness. Wincing, she waited, but there was no movement from the other end of the apartment. The sound had not woken Cristoff.

Sliding out the two large volumes by William Shakespeare, whom Cristoff had described as a revered author of the sixteenth century, she withdrew the journal. As she did, a rustle caught her ears and she remembered the scroll.

Gingerly, she felt around the back of the shelf, her cautious hand brushing the fragile parchment. Grasping it between her finger and thumb, she extracted it slowly, careful not to snag it on the rigid corners of the books.

Setting the journal next to the glass, she took the manuscript over to the window and unrolled it.

Tilting it until the moonlight fell on the surface, she was surprised to see the aged vellum covered in strange angular markings.

It was like no language she had seen before, and to try to decipher it at this time of night was unnecessary.

Hopefully, Cristoff recollects why he hid it at the back of a shelf.

She picked up the journal and her wine, and curled up in the chair by the window. Idly, she turned the pages, not reading the entries, happy simply to see Cristoff's writing. For some reason, it warmed her.

She smiled, as her train of thought careened off on a tangent. Cristoff's mastery in the bedchamber had not diminished; he still played her body with the expertise of a swordsman and the delicacy of a harpist.

The intensity of her desire for him was not quite assuaged which, unbidden, sparked another craving and her canines lengthened. She ran her tongue over the sharp tips and pondered her options.

Her smile widened.

"The delightful Madame Odeta Barreau. I do believe 'tis time I paid her a visit. A little retribution for her disrespect."

Shortly thereafter, she was in front of the address she had seen in Ioana's receipt book.

Magdalina studied the façade. It was an impressive building, clearly from an age of elegance and gentility.

Brooding over how to gain access, she murmured, "This palace is far too good for you, my dear."

She spied a side gate, which, as luck would have it, was not locked.

Gliding soundlessly through to the rear of the property, fortune continued to play favorites. A door, leading to a kind of scullery stood ajar.

"Very trusting," she murmured. "Considering the alert, I heard on that television box last week."

Following her instincts, she crossed an enormous kitchen, its walls glinting from the silvery metal accoutrements lining it. Venturing through a door at the far side, she entered a gloomy corridor.

Creeping along the thick carpet, she checked each room, none were bedchambers, her lip curling at the opulent furnishings.

"Evidently, wealth does not equate to good taste," Magdalina muttered.

She came to a large atrium, like an internal courtyard. Opposite, a huge double door, presumably the main entrance. To her right, a sweeping staircase, more suited to a ballroom than a domestic residence.

Ascending, she let her senses, and the drone of a man snoring, guide her.

Reaching an open door, she paused.

Although unlit, the room felt spacious, the shadowy shape in the middle, an enormous bed. The snoring was deafening, and Magdalina wondered how on earth either of the two people slept.

The grating noise provided the perfect cover.

Granting dominance to her vampiric nature, Magdalina walked to the head of the bed, at the side where the snoring man lay, and stared down at the couple therein.

Her mouth twisted cynically. The white silk bedding would make a lovely contrast with the blood about to be spilled and, recalling the man inside Cristoff's magic box describing her previous kill, give the people plenty of food… she grinned at her choice of phrase… for thought.

Magdalina bent over the male, she assumed was Jacques; madame's beleaguered husband.

Glancing at the pretentious harpy alongside him, Magdalina contemplated whether he was Madame Barreau's lover. A notion quickly dispelled; his essence indicated a weak male cuckolded by his wife.

You are no doubt, Jacques. She felt sorry for him… almost, and would ensure his death was quick. It was not his fault he had been blinded by Odeta's charm.

Spotting a lamp on the bedside table, Magdalina switched it on, relieved when the subdued glow did not disturb the sleepers.

Before husband or wife registered the intruder, she nipped Jacques's nose with one hand, and covered his mouth with the other.

Jacques woke with a start. Struggling for his life, he made a brave attempt to fend off his attacker, to no avail, defeated by Magdalina's superior strength.

The skirmish was brief.

His blood lacked zest, its flavour and consistency comparable with that of water, and did not quench her thirst.

Savoring the exhalation of Jacques's final breath, Magdalina was surprised at its sweetness.

Shaking that troublesome thought from her head, she rounded the bed to study his wife, unable to comprehend not only how Madame Odeta Barreau had slept through her husband's demise but also, why she wore a mask over her eyes.

Perhaps if I had to sleep next to that toad, I would do the same, so as not to see him, should I wake in the middle of night.

Unconsciously, Magdalina licked her lips as the fragrance emanating from Odeta — reminiscent of the plum syrup used, all those centuries ago, in certain desserts — teased her nostrils.

Wealth might not equate to good taste, but in your case, Odeta, it has *allowed you to age gracefully.*

She tapped the woman on the shoulder. Odeta groaned something incomprehensible and turned over. Magdalina repeated the gesture and did not stop until Odeta pushed up her mask and snapped testily, "Wha..."

Her question lodged in her throat when she met the glittering gaze of the stranger leaning over her. Something warm dripped onto her exposed skin, but she did not dare look.

"Good evening, Madame Barreau," the woman greeted, with a feline smile.

"What the f—" Odeta tried to rise, prevented by the hand on her shoulder.

Magdalina placed a light finger to Odeta's lips. "Hush, my dear, do you want to wake the dead?"

Odeta followed Magdalina's sidelong glance, her horrified gaze landing on her husband's bloodied body.

Panicking, she writhed under Magdalina's ruthless grip, and mumbled something along the lines of, "What do you want? Take it all." Her words distorted under the stranger's ice-cold finger.

Magdalina perched on the edge of the mattress. "This is a nightmare of your own making, Madame Barreau," she began conversationally. "When you treat people with contempt, there are repercussions.

"Did you think marrying into money elevated your status? Tsk, tsk, Odeta. The caliber of a person is illustrated by their behavior not their riches. Ioana has more refinement in her little finger than you can ever hope to attain.

"Do you understand?"

Odeta nodded, terrified eyes riveted on Magdalina.

"Nevertheless, I am pleased to say, you *will* achieve notoriety tonight. Are you interested to know how?"

Odeta remained as though frozen.

"You are about to become the third victim... officially... of this city's mythical vampire."

Magdalina's fiendish grin was the last thing Odeta saw.

With lightning speed, Magdalina pounced. Her fangs tore into the woman's neck severing her jugular. Blood spurted into her mouth and, instinctively, she swallowed, then leaned back to admire her handiwork in perverse fascination.

Like a fountain, blood arced in all directions, staining the white comforter deep ruby.

Satisfied, she had avenged Ioana's humiliation, Magdalina dipped her head to the gaping wound, and gorged herself.

Satiated, she let the corpse fall back against the pillows and stood. Heading for the door, she caught a glimpse of herself in the mirror.

Not in her fiercest of battles had she been soaked so thoroughly in her enemy's blood, unable to repress a disturbing swell of pride that she could take a life, indiscriminately, for no other purpose than her own pleasure.

She addressed her reflection, "I cannot return home in this condition. Dearest Odeta, may I borrow your shower to wash myself?" She tilted her head as though listening.

"Why, thank you."

Entering the bathroom, she cooed, "What's that, Madame? Feel free to help myself to one of your gowns while I am at it? Goodness, you are so generous. How could I possibly refuse?

"I must say, death *has* improved your personality."

Chapter Seventeen

All Hallows' Eve

Magdalina slid between the sheets and curled up against Cristoff, absorbing the warmth from his body. He murmured in his sleep and shifted until he could gather her close.

Content, following her nocturnal escapade, in more ways than one, Magdalina drifted off.

The aroma of coffee woke her. Stretching, hearing her bones pop and realign, she squinted at sunlight blazing through the window. "Did we not close those when we came to bed last night?" she grumbled, turning onto her stomach and burying her face in the pillow.

"Wake up, sleepy-head," a cheerful voice sang from somewhere beyond the bedroom.

"No," she groused. "Leave me alone."

"Why so grumpy?"

"I did not get much rest," Magdalina stopped short of divulging why.

Cristoff came in bearing a mug of steaming ambrosia.

The heady fragrance zapped along Magdalina's synapses, banishing her bleariness.

"Please." She shuffled upright and held out her hand, smiling when he passed her the mug. She inhaled deeply, savoring the brew.

"Nectar," she breathed, and swallowed several gulps before handing it back.

"Where did you find this?" Cristoff waved something in front of her nose.

"Give me a moment," she implored. "'Tis too early to be awake, never mind to think."

"It is after ten, lazy bones."

Magdalina blinked at him. "Surely not, it feels like only moments since I shut my eyes."

"You were out of it when I got up. Clearly your midnight jaunt was more exhausting than you anticipated." His brow quirked.

"You knew I was not beside you?"

"Of course. I always know when you are no longer near."

"Interesting," she mused, feeling the now familiar thrill glissade through her.

Setting that aside for later, she added, "In truth my… sojourn… left me weary, but it was essential." She had no need to qualify her remark. "What were you flapping in my face?"

"This. It was on the table, next to my journal. Where did you find it?" he repeated.

"Hidden behind a stack of your books." She feigned a glare. "I am not conversant with the characters, but suspect the papyrus dates to thousands of years before the AD which marks the beginning of the 'modern' era."

"The markings are called cuneiform, and this is what's known as a rubbing. The document is just a biblical reference."

"Go make me a large coffee and I'll get dressed."

"Awww… I prefer you naked, saves me ripping off your clothes." He leered lasciviously, making Magdalina giggle.

She batted him, to little effect, it must be noted.

He raised his palms. "Fine, so you are not interested in this?'" He kissed her nose. "Or this?" He kissed her shoulder. "Or this," he husked as his lips trailed a scorching path down her throat to the rise of her breast.

"We…ll," she drew out the word. "I suppose it could wait… just a little longer…" and capitulated.

Lunch was a forgotten meal by the time the couple dragged themselves out of bed. Cristoff rustled up some sandwiches and brewed a fresh pot of coffee.

"Okay," he said, after they'd eaten their fill, flattening the scroll and placing condiments on the edges to stop them from rolling up. "Basically this is a fragment of the story of Cain and Abel, the sons of Adam and Eve…"

"I know who they are," Magdalina said.

Cristoff carried on as though she had not spoken, "…and nothing to do with the dragon."

"How can you be certain?" She frowned.

"Why would anyone writing a biblical text refer to dragons?"

"I accept the premise but something prompted you to keep it. Perhaps your subconscious discerned its relevance." Magdalina shrugged. "We have nothing to lose by translating it and maybe something to gain."

"Fair enough. I'll interpret, you write."

"I am at your service, good sir." She grinned.

"Okay, ready?"

At Magdalina's nod, Cristoff, his Sumerian a little hazy, decoded the document.

"This does not deviate from the text I was taught as a child," Magdalina said when Cristoff stopped.

"Adam and Eve had two sons, one killed the other and is doomed to walk the earth for an eternity…" she trailed off.

"For an eternity," she repeated in a whisper.

"Just a minute." She read through her notes and quoted, "'The Lord said to Cain…'"

She faltered, something akin to a scream piercing her mind. She shook it off.

"'Why are you so angry and cast down? If you do well, you are accepted. If not, sin is a demon crouching at the door. It shall be eager for you and you will be mastered by it.'"

She looked at Cristoff. "A demon crouching at the door… could it be?"

He stared, his mind racing.

"And this bit, 'Now you are accursed and exiled from the ground, which has opened its mouth to receive the blood of your brother, shed by you. When you till the ground, it will no longer yield to you, its strength. You shall be an outcast.' Then further on, 'the Lord put a mark on Cain…' Ouch."

She pressed a hand to her head. "Stabbing pain," she gasped. "Too much blood maybe." Making a feeble attempt at humor.

Cristoff frowned his concern but Magdalina was already reciting her notes. "'…in order that anyone meeting him would not kill him.' Is this the answer?

"The dragon is Cain?"

As the words left her mouth, a shriek rent her skull. So loud she was sure Cristoff must hear it too.

How dare you utter my name, Thrall? You relinquished that right when you abandoned me. A reckoning looms. To defy me would be a grave mistake and lead to unimaginable devastation."

Ashen-faced, Magdalina recoiled, ice slinking down her spine. "You do not own me, fiend. We parted ways centuries ago…"

The discordant laugh which intruded, jarred her body and reverberated through her head like a waterfall of serrated metal.

"Fool. You are forever ensnared. Death is your only salvation… oh wait… you have yet to experience its release. Hahahahaha…"

The harsh rattle faded, leaving her trembling.

"Magdalina, my love, what ails you?"

She opened her eyes, her gaze colliding with Cristoff's. To her surprise, she was cradled in his arms.

"What on earth?" she asked, her words disjointed, her head still ringing.

"You collapsed. What happened?"

"It's him! We've done it, we found him. He is Cain, Cain is he. They are one and the same. Ostracized for killing his brother, he has wandered the world as a marked beast. We will find him, if I understand this correctly, where the ground has been barren since biblical times," Magdalina replied, avoiding Cristoff's question.

"What caused you to faint?" Cristoff was not to be put off.

"He has summoned me to do his bidding." She held his gaze, her expression heartbreakingly sad.

"I do not think I will be able to resist indefinitely. I am nothing more than a wielder of death. Maybe you should kill me now. Perhaps that will prevent him from executing his master plan."

"No," Cristoff retorted. "I refuse to let him win. There has to be a way for us to break this Godforsaken curse. It has to be here. The clues have to be here, somewhere in the pile of crap."

From all his research Cristoff had ascertained that, much like an alligator, a dragon had an *Achilles heel*. A small, unprotected, area at the base of its neck.

To puncture the skin at this exact spot was the *only* way to kill a dragon.

To strike it accurately the first time, required a skill even he did not possess, meaning the prospect of success lay somewhere between unlikely and impossible.

He could not bring himself to tell Magdalina, their quest was hopeless.

Resigning himself to it being their only chance, he said, "Please meet me at the car. I need to grab a manuscript which may help us locate him."

"*Excuse* me?"

"According to this text… there is only one place he might reside."

"Chris, you *know* how I feel about that ugly contraption. Give me one good reason why I should climb into it to risk life and limb, on the possibility of a maybe?"

"Have you mastered the powers of transportation? If not, we have no other—"

"Wait… trans what?"

Cristoff spun her about and swatted her on the ass, causing a startled yelp.

Rubbing her butt, she glared at him over her shoulder. "You could have just said please."

"I already did, to no avail. Now, scoot."

Sticking her tongue out at him, she sauntered out of the apartment, slamming the door behind her.

Mesmerized, as always, by the sight of her svelte frame sashaying in front of him, Cristoff stood alone in the silence.

Of course, it would have to be today. Apparently, even dragons are suckers for the hype.

Collecting his thoughts, he gathered everything he had on Transylvania and the Hoia Baciu Forest from his desk.

Then, he pressed a button opening a hidden compartment beneath the center drawer.

Nestled within, a weapon he had not used since the tragic day this all began; fated to be restored to him by his unsuspecting queen. He picked it up, the weight in his hand, reassuring. It might not do the trick, but it was worth the try.

Sliding it into a sheath, which he strapped to his belt, Cristoff glanced around the apartment, closed the door, and went to join Magdalina in the car for the long ride ahead.

Chapter Eighteen

Nothing in Magdalina's life prepared her for the experience of hurtling along at breakneck speed, in a metal box.

Even her favorite steed had not the pace to outrun this wheeled monster. The account of the steam train in Cristoff's journal, popped into her head… *oh hell, no.*

She failed to notice or appreciate the irony that, not only did the car share the historical name of her kingdom — the protection of which began in antiquity when her ancestor swore fealty to a dragon — but also, it was delivering her back to the same winged revenant.

As the towns and villages, most of which did not exist under the former queen's rule, whizzed by, she muttered to any deity who might be sympathetic, "If you are listening and have *any* compassion, now might be a good time to safeguard me from certain death."

Other than a brief interlude during which Cristoff deemed it necessary to explain the internal combustion engine to her — for reasons the poor woman could not fathom, unaware it was a calculated tactic to deflect her attention — they had barely spoken for five hours.

Cristoff was concentrating on the unlit road, and Magdalina feared speaking might distract him, resulting in him losing control of the car, swerving off the road, and crashing in a blazing inferno.

They only stopped once en route, and that was to feed the diabolical chariot.

With the vehicle stationary, Magdalina strove to calm her erratic heartbeat and relax her death grip on the papers she was perusing, conscious their state was more fragile than hers.

Regaining a degree of equanimity, she leaned back in her seat and took several deep breaths while Cristoff finished his task and went inside the building.

He returned with an armful of drinks and food, none of which his passenger refused, despite being concerned she would lose the contents of her stomach as he lurched back onto the road.

Seeing a sign for the Hoia Baciu Forest, Cristoff broke the uneasy quiet.

"We are about an hour away."

Magdalina found her voice, "Why could this not wait until sunrise? It will be the middle of the night when we get there."

For the first time since they departed Bucharest, Cristoff eased off the accelerator and, as they cruised along at a far more sensible rate, glanced across at Magdalina.

"I do not believe we could delay. You know what the date is?"

Magdalina shook her head. As with marking the hours in the day, the calendar was only useful to delineate the seasons.

"It is thirty-first of October. All Hallow's Eve. The night

when the boundary between the worlds of the living and the dead become blurred. What better night?" He did not elaborate.

"You said you heard the dragon cry out when you suggested its name was Cain. I'm astonished he is *that* old. I guess punishing him for killing his brother in a jealous rage was not enough... God transformed him into an immortal dragon to boot."

"How can we be certain?" Magdalina queried. "The information we are relying on, came from a scrap of parchment *you* rejected and left to decay in that jumble of books you call a library. You can thank me for finding it."

"Right after we have a conversation about *your* refusal to give me my journal. It's been with me for so long, it's become a part of me."

"When was your last entry?" Magdalina retorted. "Let me remind you. Nineteen forty-four, nearly five decades ago. Did you ever consider that perhaps *your* recent neglect of the poor thing left it thinking you were dead again? I would hate to travel to some English bookstore to reclaim it every other day," she exaggerated, rolling her eyes in emphasis.

Conceding his cherished journal was lost to him... for now, Cristoff changed the subject as he changed gears, aware Magdalina's desire to argue about something as insignificant, in the grand scheme of things, as his diary was to take her mind off what lay ahead.

"How was I to know an incomplete stone rubbing of a story which paralleled the book of Genesis would reveal the answer?"

"Mayhap by reading it assiduously, Doctor Williamson..."

It was some time since she had used his title.

"...any archaeologist who discards a seven-hundred year old rubbing from a four thousand year old Sumerian cuneiform tablet deserves to be throttled. In your defense, we do not know whether the translation is based on truth because, apparently, the tablet was carved two thousand years after the fact."

"And brings us to why we are racing across Romania in the middle of the night. You were summoned by the creature no sooner had the word left your lips. Are you afraid to face him and finish this? Has our search been for naught?"

"*No*," Magdalina growled, masking her trepidation. "He will know his defeat and my freedom this night."

Cristoff wove the car through the Transylvanian city of Cluj-Napoca, passed the imposing Orthodox Cathedral, relieved when he spotted the sign for Hoia Baciu.

Several minutes of winding roads, and they turned onto the Strada Donath, which led, apparently, to some of the main walking tracks.

Unable to determine whether there was a designated parking zone, Cristoff drove along until the road… such as it was… petered out into a what looked like a goat trail.

The site was eerily quiet. Tonight, of all nights, Chris expected the place to be teeming with ghost hunters, but there was not another soul abroad.

A blessing?

Maybe.

Chris was under no illusion as to why, coincidentally, the forest was deserted — they were expected.

Steeling himself, he angled the car so the beams from the headlights illuminated the imposing landscape. The bright arc did not penetrate far and only made the forest appear even more ominous.

Determined to gain as much insight into her enemy as

time allowed, Magdalina had spent the majority of the journey immersed in the documents, Cristoff had thought to bring, regarding their destination.

The forest, she had gleaned from the texts, was considered by those declaring themselves the oracles of all things paranormal, to be one of the most haunted in the world. Rife with ghosts, demons, and the home of the Devil himself.

In the center, a near perfect oval designated as *The Clearing*. A place where, since before recorded time, nothing had grown and, for which, to date, scientists could supply no explanation.

Magdalina knew.

She could feel it in her very core.

It concealed the portal to *his* lair.

Cristoff's hand came to rest on Magdalina's knee. "Are you ready?" he asked softly.

Magdalina could only nod in response.

He leaned over to brush a gentle kiss to her lips, allowing it to linger, hoping to boost her confidence that they would be victorious.

Breaking from his warmth, Magdalina leveled an anxious gaze at him.

"Promise me, Cristoff. You will stay by my side. No matter what."

"Without hesitation, my Queen. I shall not fail you again."

She opened the car door, whispering, "Never in your life, in all of your lives, have you failed me."

The two alighted, and paused in front of the Dacia. Cristoff had left the lights on, anticipating they would provide a clearer field of view.

Regrettably, the mist emanating from the depths of the trees created a foreboding shroud around the interior.

Flicking on his torch, Cristoff clasped Magdalina's hand,

and the two ventured forward. Between the trees and the fog, they were soon separated from the artificial security of the car's headlights, and quite alone.

Doggedly, they trod the ancient path, avoiding the clawing branches of twisted limbs, coming out at the heart of Hoia Baciu. True to the legend, it was a barren spot.

The reek of tainted blood and decay, assaulted Magdalina's senses. The putrid odor brought her to a dead standstill, awakening her thirst.

Unable to stop herself, she released Cristoff's hand — inverting *his* promise not to desert *her* — and darted to the middle of the clearing.

Dropping to her knees, she beseeched wretchedly, "P-Please, m-my love, flee. I-I cannot contain myself. Y-You should not be here."

Desperately, she fought the impulse to lunge at Cristoff and tear out his throat as her craving intensified.

Stubbornly, he refused to move. Magdalina's agonized expression cementing his resolve not abandon her… ever again.

Instead, he joined her in the oval and commanded, "Summon the bastard."

Placing her palms on the dead soil, Magdalina threw back her head to look up at the night sky, and howled, "We are here at your bidding. Grant us passage."

A thunderous rumble shook the forest. Without warning, the ground opened beneath them, and they plunged headlong into nothingness.

The last thing Magdalina saw above her was the ground swallowing the moon.

Darkness surrounded them. Each breath was laboured, the air suffocatingly dense with the noxious odor of brimstone.

A spark at the far end of the murkiness, ignited the sulfur particles in the air, generating a flash fire.

Magdalina thought their end was at hand, only to realize they were engulfed in a protective cocoon. The fire raged around them, but the dragon ensured it did not devour his guests.

Morphing into human form, while maintaining his obsidian-hued flesh, the dragon circled them slowly, hands clasped behind his back like a cantankerous Greek academic considering his words before chastising his student for a foolish error.

Cristoff rose and helped Magdalina to her feet; the pair keeping watchful eyes on their host.

Finally, the dragon spoke, "I am glad to see you have abandoned your refusal to accept your fate, Thrall."

"I never agreed to your terms." Magdalina's chin went up defiantly.

"Yet, here you are, with a sacrifice no less. In reward for your submission, I shall allow you to terminate his irritating existence once and for all.

"Although, I *do* extend my thanks, Cristoff, for recovering her body. What those fools did to her was not part of our agreement."

"I did not do anything for your benefit, devil," Cristoff refuted.

"Perhaps not, but that does not alter the outcome. Debts require payment."

Stepping closer to one of the walls, the dragon illuminated countless handprints decorating the coarse surface.

Cristoff sucked in a breath, acknowledging their similarity to those found in the Pech Merle cave in France.

At Cristoff's stunned expression, the dragon flashed a toothy grin, taunting, "Do you believe them to be crude works of ancient art, as your learned colleagues attest? Errantly, I might add. At least you can die knowing the truth of their origins."

The demon ran a hand over the jagged surface. "These represent lives sworn to serve my depravity. Like your gullible ancestor, Decebalus. All it took was for me to hint at unheard of wealth and power, and they were only too eager to sell their souls, ignoring the caveat that there is no such thing as a free ride. Simple checks and balances."

With a shrug, he chided, "The Devil is in the details, is it not? As the human phrase goes, *you cannot take it with you*."

"How can that be?" Cristoff's astonishment echoed around the cavern. "These prints are tens of thousands of years old."

"Yes, *Cain*…" Magdalina broke in, hoping the appellation might inflict a fatal wound or, at the bare minimum, hurt him. "You are only—"

"My dear child, evil such as I, is ageless. Believing I am a character in that fairytale amuses me."

"I heard your yowl of pain when I spoke your name."

He studied them, meditatively. "Would you have come had I not? Enough, let us end this useless conversation. You," he looked at Magdalina, "and I have business to conclude.

"While I cannot guarantee your accommodation will be as luxurious as the good doctor's abode, it will be preferable to a coffin in freezing water."

Twirling his finger, he forced Magdalina to face Cristoff, "Magdalina Dragoš, kill your lover and seal our covenant."

She felt her body move of its own volition. Her lips parted, exposing her fangs, her hunger insatiable.

The dragon had witnessed this scene more times than he

cared to remember, and averted his head, not from abhorrence, but apathy.

Cristoff watched the remnants of his beloved's humanity vanish from her eyes.

Her words slurring, she fought the corrupted compulsion, "K-Kill... me... Cristoff. Do not let me turn on you."

He allowed her to advance. When she was barely an inch from him, he retrieved the ancient blade from the sheath on his belt. Not even Magdalina was aware of it.

As her teeth grazed his throat, Cristoff hurled the dagger with all his might. The finely honed steel sank deep into the base of the dragon's neck; Cristoff's aim, savagely accurate.

The strike did not vanquish the dragon, but the shooting pain caused him to lose focus on his spell, bringing the protective walls down around them.

Flames engulfed the trio.

A blood-curdling howl, which echoed back to the dawn of time, erupted from the dragon as he was sucked into the fathomless bowels of Hell. Magdalina's refusal to submit, revoking the curse.

Perhaps love did conquer evil.

Magdalina in his arms, Cristoff choked his dying promise, "I will find you in my next life."

All Saints' Day

The glistening dew had not yet evaporated when Andrei, the first of the staff, drove into Hoia Baciu the next morning. Tendrils of mist hovered above the trees, as the rays from the autumn sun warmed the earth.

It was Andrei's job to check the tracks before the tourist groups arrived. Given the tales associated with the forest, it had become something of a mecca for paranormal enthusiasts, and it was not unusual to find hikers setting up camp, in hopes of witnessing supernatural activity.

Halloween attracted them in droves.

Andrei was not surprised to see a car parked facing the forest. He *was* surprised to see it was the only one. *Odd, have the rest scarpered already?* "Frightened off by the ghouls." He chuckled.

As he came to a halt, he saw the car's doors standing open, and that the headlights had been left on, reduced to the merest flicker as the beam faded with the battery.

Alighting, he noticed, with consternation, tiny beads of water blanketing the vehicle. It had been parked here all night.

"Damn kids," he grumbled. "Always think they can debunk the myth. Not happened yet."

Annoyed at having to tramp through the damp forest to check on the fools, Andrei locked his car and, pulling up his collar to stave off the frosty air, set off. Glancing at his watch, he probably had a good hour before he was required to assist tourists.

Fingers of sunlight pierced the gloom of the forest, pushing back the shadows.

Occasionally, he "Cooeee'd", but there was no answering cry, not even one for help.

Andrei came to *The Clearing*.

The ground looked to have been disturbed and there was a faint odor of bonfire, mixed with sulfur.

Frowning, he skirted the huge space, but there was no sign of footprints, nor any indication that pesky paranormal investigators had passed this way.

Turning to leave, his steps were halted by an abnormality right in the center of the arid circle.

A green stem — not very big, but definitely flourishing.

"You have *got* to be kidding." Andrei whistled incredulously, then galloped back to his car, bursting with the news.

The owners of the abandoned car were never traced.

Epiloque

September 2022

The battered coach disgorged its passengers who chatted animatedly while waiting for the driver to unload their equipment from the luggage bay.

"So nice to be back, without restrictions," one of their number said, to nods all around.

The last two years had been… challenging for the countless archaeological teams across the world. Access to the majority of sites currently under excavation had been limited, or in some cases denied altogether.

Protecting the population from the virus took precedence over preserving artifacts.

Adjusting to changes in certain standards had thrown the occasional spanner in the works but, for the most part, life had returned to normal.

To everyone's relief.

"Come on people, the bus won't unpack itself." A woman with blue and purple streaks in her black hair, an olive complexion, sloe eyes and an air of authority, began directing operations.

Dr. Albescu was notorious in the field of archaeology, not only for her uncanny ability to discover sites thought lost to history, but also for her engaging manner. Those who studied under her, alleged she could make even the driest topic magical.

They would soon see whether that was true.

A tall, craggy-featured man with an unruly mop of dark-brown hair under a weather-beaten Akubra, and shrewd green eyes, shouldered his backpack and picked up a box of tools. The deep bronze of his skin spoke of years working in the field.

"You are?" Dr. Albescu demanded.

"Doctor Chris Standish." He grinned affably.

The older woman laughed. "Well whaddya know? I used to have a dog called Doctor Chris. She was a stray, a family friend brought home one night. My mother could not understand why I insisted on giving a female dog a boy's name."

She slapped the man on his shoulder. "Mind, I won't be spoiling you laggards like I spoiled that dog, bless her paws." Still laughing, she wandered off to a group of students who looked totally out of their depths.

An image of a much younger Dr. Albescu flickered in the man's head only to vanish before he could decide whether it was a memory or his imagination.

Dismissing it as nonsense, he strolled over to the entrance and tilted his head, using his hat to shield his eyes from the dazzling Romanian sun, to look up at the ruined structure.

Hidden for a millennium, the site was revealed after a recent wildfire destroyed the surrounding forest.

The previous year, Dr Albescu, who had argued for its

existence in her doctoral thesis, led the first team granted permits to map the remains. The excavations had uncovered a plethora of tantalizing finds dating to the final days of the last ruling dynasty.

The hope was, with the new technologies available, this dig would be able to peel back the layers, to unearth evidence relating to the House of Dragoš, prior to its collapse.

The soaring walls of the once mighty ramparts had long since crumbled or been appropriated centuries ago by locals desperate for building material, but the internal footprint of the stronghold was clearly visible.

History told of a crusade against a formidable queen who was defeated and murdered by her enemies, her body never found.

Myth whispered of demons and magic, and degenerate practices contrary to the Orthodox faith, and the justification for eradicating the family from the face of the earth.

Truth, undoubtedly, lay closer to the former than the latter, and one of the goals of this season was to gather enough material to separate fact from fiction.

Other than the initial dig, the site was pristine. As far as the experts could determine, it had never been looted. Superstition enough to deter greedy treasure hunters.

The scuff of footsteps prompted the man to turn and smile at the woman approaching him, hand on her hat to stop it slipping off her head as she mirrored his stance.

He smiled affably, thinking she was one of the most beautiful women he had ever seen. Her rumpled clothing and sadly maligned wide-brimmed hat…. which would probably not survive the next few weeks… could not disguise her slender figure and tanned yet delicate countenance.

In her hands she clutched a shabby-looking book. Something about it, teased at his subconscious.

Putting that on the back-burner, he introduced himself, "Hi, I'm Chris, part of the Durham university contingent, good to meet you. Given the rumors attached to the fortress, this is going to be an interesting dig."

"Right… battles and dragons, vampires and curses. Some kind of corrupt covenant don't they say? I love a good legend." The woman grinned her enthusiasm, her brilliant blue eyes sparkling in the summer sunshine. "Hard to imagine on a day like this, mind."

She waved the book under his nose. "Talking about legends, I found this in a lovely old book shop in London, tucked behind the Romania tourist guidebook, I was after. So strange don't you think, what you find when you least expect to?"

He didn't answer, assuming her remark to be rhetorical. Confirmed seconds later.

"Anyway, it's fascinating. It's a journal, one begun in eighteen hundred. Can you imagine, eighteen hundred? It documents the writer's investigations into the stories surrounding this old fortress, mostly related to ancient manuscripts he tracked down.

"It's also a timeline of events, clearly important to the original author and subsequent diarists. Absolutely riveting. Weird though, the entries continue right up to nineteen forty-four then stop suddenly, right in the middle of a word actually.

"That's nearly two hundred years. Cool, huh? I wondered whether it was something that had been passed down through his family… the writing doesn't alter much… but there's no name. Given the ragged edge of paper where the flyleaf should be, I daresay some idiot tore it out. No respect."

The woman did not bother to hide her scorn for the culprit.

"When my faculty asked for expressions of interest for this year's excavation, I jumped at the chance. Fate… has to be." She winked. "I know it's a long shot but, if even one piece of evidence matches his findings, it would be the cherry on the top of a very tasty cake, don't you reckon?"

Her impish grin tugged on the periphery of his consciousness. "Wanna take a look?" She offered him the journal.

Chris had to control the urge to snatch the book out of her grasp. "Thank you."

Their fingers brushed as he accepted the journal, eliciting a curious prickle of recognition

Neither commented.

Chris opened the book carefully, the cover creaking with age, the pages yellowed and brittle. The writing was hauntingly familiar and, as he peered at the fading entries, a feeling of coming home settled over him. Not the time… but hopefully soon.

Leaving him with the journal, the woman stepped closer to the walls.

Something glinted in the dust and she bent to pick it up. "Goodness, we've barely set foot on the site, and already…" She did not need to finish her sentence.

On her palm lay a large splinter of dulled glass. Rubbing it between her fingers to remove a thick layer of dust, she raised it up so the light shone through it.

It was a deep ruby red.

A picture flashed through her mind, of a dragon holding a white shield smeared with blood, so quickly she dismissed it as imagination.

She looked at Chris, a frisson of something tantalizingly elusive skating down her spine. Ignoring it, she handed him the shard.

"Very interesting indeed, and my name is Magda."

Please don't leave just yet…
Enjoy these short extras!

A
Little
Extra

VIII

JUSTICE

Justice

Henry Moore sat in his chair, waiting for his blasted number to be announced. He hated mixing with these lower forms of life, let alone being obliged to do so at the Department of Motor Vehicles.

This was more than he could tolerate.

Mentally, he wrote a scathing review, which he would take great delight in posting to all his social media accounts when he got home.

He glanced at the letter from the State, granting the return of his driving privileges.

Privileges indeed, he scoffed to himself, before turning to the attractive but somewhat pale woman sitting quietly next to him.

Being, in effect, a captive audience, she seemed the best candidate on whom to level his discontent with the entire DMV system.

"This is absurd, don't you agree?" Moore started querulously.

Of course, he did not let the poor woman answer. "This fucking state steals millions from us in taxes, and then expects us to sit here *patiently* for the next window to open, so we can get fleeced, yet again, by the greedy vultures."

The ashen-faced woman twisted slightly, to study Moore with sullen eyes before returning her gaze to the numbers scrolling slowly on the overhead screen, apparently content to sit and wait for her number in silence.

"Now Serving D Six-Two-Five at Window Eleven," the hollow, computerized voice announced, accompanied by an annoying background buzz, which made Moore's teeth grind every time he heard it.

"D Six-Two-Five," Moore echoed. "I've been sitting here for two hours. *Two hours, I say*," he raised his voice as though doing so would accelerate the process and get him out of this hell. He hoped it might spark a reaction from his taciturn companion who appeared unwilling to join in his tirade.

"They haven't even called any of the B tickets in, at least…," he looked at his watch, "…half an hour. I'm sure of it. I feel like I'm in line at a damned butcher's shop. Don't they know we all have better things to do than waste our days watching them take continuous coffee breaks," he grumbled.

The woman next to him, let out a forlorn sigh. Her eyes glued to the screen, she replied, softly, "They're busy. I'm sure they will get to us as quickly as they can."

"Bah," Moore scoffed. "If they had more people working at the counters and fewer people pushing papers…" he paused for a moment, purposely leaving the woman hanging anxiously for his next profound observation, "…instead of filling offices at the State Capital, pushing the exact same ridiculous paperwork as this, we unfortunate citizens would not have to suffer this farce."

Moore waved the document at the woman. When she turned away from that damn screen to look at it, the trickle of triumph told him he had her in the palm of his hand.

"Two thousand dollars. That's what this paper cost me,

not to mention my license for a year, and lawyers' fees, and why, you ask? Why indeed? I certainly was *not* driving under the influence. I've drunk more at dinner parties plenty of times and never had a problem driving. I'll bet that cop was just looking to pad out his quotas for DUI arrests."

The woman's tired eyes scrutinized him again. "Drinking and driving is illegal."

"It's only illegal if you can't handle your alcohol, dear woman," Moore assured her, "and I, for one, have no problem doing so."

The woman canted her head.

Moore stared as, oddly it appeared to tilt more to one side than was possible. In fact, her head did not seem to sit properly on her shoulders at all.

She repeated the same public service announcement, "Drinking and driving is illegal," adding, "People can get hurt, or die."

Moore spoke as though she had not interjected, *typical bleeding heart*, "Do you have any idea how frustrating it is to ask for rides… *everywhere*… not to mention what it costs me in cab fares and limo rides?

"Good God, I'm positive I have paid to educate *those people's* kids," indicating the customer service representatives at the windows, with an infuriated gesture. "Hell, I probably sent them all to medical school.

"Oh, and don't get me started on what I think about this State's *generous* medical policies to those foreigners.

"Now… *now*… the State has seen fit to return my license. A privilege, they say. It's my **goddamn** right to have a license, I say. I've been driving since I was fourteen. If I happen to have a drink or two before I get behind the wheel, well, that's my *privilege*."

"Drinking and driving is illegal," the woman stated flatly, as though she was stuck in a loop.

"Now Serving A Twenty-Nine at Window Two," the computerized voice droned.

The woman appeared wholly unmoved by Moore's speech, which exacerbated his outrage. He had a cogent point to make, and was damned if he wouldn't make her agree.

Moore figured he might get more sympathy if he elaborated on the reason for his miserable trip here today.

"Yes, dear lady, I appreciate your point, but when invited to a fundraiser for the man who should be Governor of our fair State, who am I to decline?

"Yes, cocktails were served, but I know my limits. I'm betting the damn cop was sent to spy on the party and harass any of the guests who dare oppose our *mighty* Governor. Obviously, this is nothing but a sham."

The part of his story, Moore had, conveniently, left out concerned the car he nearly hit when he drifted over the yellow line. He classed it as immaterial because his lawyer had managed to keep the incident from ever going to Court.

He was acquitted of causing the accident. It was humiliating enough to be required to attend the closed door meeting in the judge's quarters.

Besides, the woman was found guilty of *Distracted Driving*; the legal term cited by his lawyer.

They had found a text on her phone which could have occurred at the same time as the incident. *Contributory Negligence* was the other term his lawyer used. It helped to have the best attorney money could buy.

"Now Serving B Two-Seven-Eight at Window Fourteen," the computer voice sang.

"*Finally,*" Moore sniped dramatically. His attention switched from his companion to the television screen and over to the relevant window.

The automated voice repeated, "Now Serving B Two-Seven-Eight at Window Fourteen."

Moore broke into a new rant about the nerve of DMV, expecting him to jump to attention and run to the appropriate window after they had dared make him wait so long. He was still complaining when he turned to wish the long-suffering woman good luck in her wait.

To his surprise, she had vanished. He glanced around to see whether she had moved or was at one of the windows, but she was nowhere to be seen.

"Fuck you too, lady," Henry Moore grumbled. "No one has manners anymore."

Moore stomped across to the window with his required documentation, triple checked before leaving home. He was not about to let them stall proceedings on a technicality about some obscure scrap of paper which no one had told him was important.

The young man at the counter looked over the stack of legal forms Moore had shoved across the counter at him.

Moore watched him flip through the pages, slowly and deliberately.

"Yes, yes, I assure you, it's all in order." Moore made an effort to mask his disdain.

"I'm sure it is, sir, but I have to check it all the same," the young man replied, without lifting his eyes.

There was something oddly familiar about the man's face, but Moore couldn't place it. He was sure he had seen him somewhere before, despite the man having no remarkable features.

Maybe, Moore thought, *we are members of the same church.*

He was, of course, an upstanding member of his congregation. In fact, he was a Deacon of the flock *and* attended services every week.

Who knows? The congregation is pretty large. I doubt even the preacher could keep track of all those unprepossessing people anyway.

"All right, sir," the young man interrupted Moore mid-thought, "If you will excuse me for a moment, I need to contact the Control Department so I—"

"It says right there on that sheet, I can take this test today," Moore snapped. "I have no idea what issue you have with my paperwork. Do you know your job or do I need to speak to your supervisor?"

The young man's jaw stiffened. "It's standard procedure, sir. The Department has to open your record for us to continue."

Aggrieved at yet another delay, Moore huffed as the man went about his business.

The discussion with the Control Department was brief and, within moments, the man at the counter had entered Moore's information.

Set for another confrontation with Moore, the young man explained, as calmly as he could, "That will be $7.50 for the permit test."

Given the amount of money he had already shelled out on legal fees just to get to this point, Moore considered adding a grievance to his pending review, about being nickeled and dimed in order to re-sit a test, he should not have to take.

The pair stared each other down from opposite sides of the counter. Finally, Moore bit his tongue, swallowed his pride, and paid the man.

Moore had not bothered to read the driver's manual, assuming the test had not changed much since the last time he took it, forty something years ago.

An error he was about to realize.

The topics bore no resemblance to the simple *Identify the Shape* questions he dealt with so easily as a teenager. No, these scenarios required thought and math, as well as sobering questions related to *Drink Driving*.

Moore was convinced he had been given this particular test, deliberately, not only so he would fail, but also to make him feel guilty. By pure fluke, he guessed the last answer correctly, and passed the theory portion of the examination.

Estimating the distance between cars... preposterous, he bitched silently at the screen.

Jubilantly, Moore returned to the counter as instructed by the soulless display. He had shown these pathetic, bureaucratic bastards, Henry Moore could not be defeated and would win the God given right to get his license back.

The only thing left to contend with was his driving test. He had been driving for decades. It was about time these poor saps witnessed an expert behind the wheel.

The young man at the counter completed Moore's paperwork for his permit, and braced himself for the anticipated outburst; startled when Moore slapped down a second $7.50 for the permit without comment.

The third $7.50, the man charged for the driving test did not receive the same understanding.

"Jesus, Joseph, and Mary. I *just* paid you fifteen dollars for this worthless piece of plastic, I'm not even going to keep once I pass this damned road test," Moore argued, waving his newly minted permit in the customer service man's face.

"If that is not insulting enough, you want to charge me **again** to take yet another test?" Moore expostulated.

"Yes, sir, and once you pass your driving test, you will have to pay for your license in full," the man's voice teetered on exasperation at the necessity of explaining this same point, over and over again.

"Fucking rip off, if ever I've heard one," Moore snarled, pulling out his credit card to pay. "Do not think the Governor will avoid an earful either."

As was his habit whenever this situation arose — frequently — the young man ignored the snide comment and finished the paperwork.

Collecting the documentation, he told Moore to take a seat, and a tester would be along shortly. Without waiting to see whether Moore obeyed, he left the counter.

With no alternative but to do as instructed, Moore gaped at the employee's apparent insolence.

He slumped onto an uncomfortable DMV chair, his hopes of voicing his latest criticism of this place on yet another unsuspecting victim, dashed when he realized he was alone.

Moore made do with mentally berating all those who had any hand in this travesty until a voice hailed him, "Henry Moore."

He looked up to see the same, disrespectful, employee clutching a clipboard, saying something about his car and starting the engine. Moore rose from his seat and led the man out.

It was Henry Moore's time to shine.

The two reached Moore's vehicle, where he proceeded to demonstrate his ability to operate the lights and wipers. Moore was tempted to roll his eyes when asked to honk the horn, but refrained; surmising, correctly as it happened, this would not do him any favors.

The vehicle check complete, the young man climbed into the front passenger seat and recited the well-rehearsed spiel concerning directions for the test. He stopped every so often to ensure Moore understood.

Then he directed Moore to execute a parallel park.

It took Moore two attempts to maneuver his Cadillac

into the space. He grumbled about the futility of this exercise, stating *nobody* parallel parked anymore, but it fell on deaf ears.

Seemingly unfazed by the censure, the young man instructed Moore to head for the exit of the parking lot and the next portion of the exam… the Road Test.

Confident he was on the home stretch for the reinstatement of his license, Moore bit his tongue.

Once we return to this crappy office, I will be seeking out his superior so I can report this insufferable prick's execrable attitude.

Tipped off by his lawyer about the circuit the test followed, Moore knew which direction he would be expected to take at certain intersections. When the young man did *not* ask him to turn left as anticipated, he was confused.

"Shouldn't we have turned there?" Moore asked.

"Now how could you know that, Mr. Moore?" the man inquired with a sharp glance. "Yes, you are correct, normally we take the left there but, due to your driving history, we are required to extend the Road Test…" he paused, "…slightly."

Moore stared at the road, anger flaring at this unforeseen development. Another complaint to add to his everincreasing list.

The next left… the next right… continue straight… the next left…there was something strangely familiar about the scenery as they traveled the route.

At the last intersection, Moore recognized the road he was on. His eyes shot to the young man who was staring straight ahead.

"**Why the fuck have you brought me here?**" Moore roared. "***Do you hear me, you bastard? Why are we on this road?***"

"I'm glad to see you remember where we are," the young man said softly, "I was afraid you might not because this time, you are sober."

"I don't know what sick game you are playing. When we get back to the DMV, I will ensure you are fired, *and* arrested for kidnap," Moore barked as he accelerated, wanting to get off this particular road as fast as possible.

"Wasn't it about here, Kaylie?" Moore heard the man ask.

"Kaylie? Who the hell is Kaylie? Are you off your rocker?" Moore retorted.

"Oh, how rude of me," the young man answered. "I forgot you two never met… officially.

"Allow me to introduce my sister, Kaylie Jordan. The woman *you* murdered that night when you ran her off the road, then abandoned her."

"What the fuck are you—" Moore stopped, his attention lifting to the mirror to see what the young man was looking at.

His face leached of all color.

Sitting in the backseat, the same woman to whom he had been venting his spleen at the DMV.

Her eyes were no longer listless, as she glared at Moore through the mirror, they seemed to burn with hatred.

Fear gripped him, but he could not avert his gaze.

He felt the car weave uncontrollably within his hands, but he remained as though frozen, locked in the woman's stare. He even heard the blare of horns as cars swerved to avoid the Cadillac.

"Yes, Henry Moore," the young man lectured, "you may have escaped the justice of the living, but the dead always find a way to even the score."

Those were the last words Henry Moore heard as he watched the woman lean forward. He felt her cold hands grip his head and jerk it backwards with unimaginable strength.

The large car skidded off the road, and slammed into an

old oak tree growing on the verge. The front grill melding itself around the trunk.

The EMTs who removed Moore's body from the vehicle noted the cause of death as a broken neck, no doubt due to the force of the impact.

As the passenger was transferred to the ambulance, a patrolman asked him why they had strayed so far from the normal test route.

"I don't know, Officer. I told him to take the left, but he carried straight on, and ignored my instructions," young man answered, wide-eyed.

"Had to fail him, of course, and I guess he just went crazy. It was weird though, he kept looking in the mirror, like he saw a ghost, or something chasing him. I've never seen anything like it."

His eyes on the mangled wreck, the patrolman scratched his head in bemusement, "You're lucky to be alive. This road is notorious for bad accidents."

His sister's reflection flickered in the glass of the ambulance door as the EMT shut it. Her expression, one of resolution, and her sweet smile let him know she was at peace.

"I guess my guardian angel was with me. Too bad I can't say the same for him."

XX

JUDGEMENT

Judgement

Jackson had spent the last 150 years lumbering through Purgatory; although, to him, it was more like being shuffled through a disorganized bureaucracy.

The bleakness of the surrounding plains had done little to relieve the misery of the wait and, despite… finally… reaching the Gates of Hell, even admission here was not guaranteed.

A short, rotund and bespectacled man perched behind the desk, thumbing through a stack of papers, seemed to be in charge of this circus and Jackson's eternity.

He addressed the newest arrival without looking up.

"Randal Jackson, five foot nine, family man, blah, blah, blah." The Gatekeeper discarded the file on his desk.

Assessing Jackson, he pushed his horn rimmed glasses up to the bridge of his nose, and gave him a quick once over before continuing. "Do you have any idea to whom you are speaking?"

Jackson dropped his gaze and murmured, "The Devil?"

The Gatekeeper laughed. "Hardly, you fool.

"I am the One who decides whether you spend eternity in

a cushy corner office filing paperwork, or chained to the blast furnace stoking coal so our Gate maintains its glitter.

"I confess, after reading your ridiculously boring file, I cannot fathom what you have done to end up here?

"A tip… your story should be brief and entertaining because, for millennia, I've heard all the lies which could ever be told, and that line behind you isn't going to process itself."

As though seeking inspiration, Jackson glanced over his shoulder at the unending parade of the damned.

Directly behind him, a naked woman with a gunshot wound, bristled with irritation. Jackson, who had no idea what she was upset about, besides being shot and finding herself in this miserable line, chalked up her vexed demeanour to impatience.

Beyond her loitered an odd-looking gentleman who peered around the woman occasionally. He too appeared to lack any clothing, but Jackson could not be certain.

Interestingly, his expression mirrored that of the woman.

With a shrug, Jackson turned back to the Gatekeeper. Scuffing the brimstone with the toe of his shoe, he corralled the facts in his mind.

Putting on his bravest face, he began his story.

"Sir, I married my wife when I was very young. An arrangement between our two families, based on the under-standing that, in exchange for my bride, I worked for her father's insurance agency, learning the ropes. Eventually, he would make me a partner, and leave the company to me when he retired.

"That was the plan. In reality, he worked me like a dog day and night. I was nothing more than a glorified bean count—" Jackson registered what he was about to say.

The scowl on the Gatekeeper's face, informed Jackson he was about to step on a landmine.

"Err… anyway, the old goat delivered a real slap in the

face, and left the blasted company to my free-loading brother-in-law. All my efforts, wasted.

"Honestly, the deadbeat never spent a single day in the office. I threatened to quit, to discover my parents had sold me to my father-in-law in perpetual servitude ."

Jackson drew a breath to curb his aggravation.

"My home life was no better. My wife refused to get a job and spent every penny I earned. If I warned her I'd cut her off financially, she ignored me or threatened to have one of her boyfriends beat me up."

He kicked at a burning ember. "One day I could not take it anymore. I purchased a gun from a pawn shop during lunch, then went to a bar and got plenty liquored up to make sure I did not lose my nerve.

"It was late by the time I got home and the house was in darkness, but I didn't need the lights because I could hear them in our bedroom.

"By all that's sacred, in our own marriage bed no less. Hand on heart can you blame me for wanting to end my suffering?

"I burst through the door and started firing. I heard an extra shot, I couldn't account for, which might explain my current predicament."

Taking off his glasses, the Gatekeeper rubbed the bridge of his nose as he contemplated the story.

"You are correct, Mr. Jackson, the extra shot came from the constable who caught you in the middle of your hunting expedition. The police were summoned when the next-door neighbour saw a strange man breaking into his friend's house."

He opened a drawer in his massive mahogany desk and retrieved a key. Handing it to Jackson, he chuckled. "You'll find your office at the end of the hall to the right."

Unwilling to question his final judgment, Jackson was

puzzled, "W-while I appreciate your decision, I-I do not understand it."

"You broke into the wrong house and shot the wrong couple. Anyone who could screw up that badly has a future in Hell's Human Resources. Please get to work."

The Gatekeeper shouted, "*Next.*"

Picking up the pertinent folder, he saw the name of a man and woman, neither sharing the same last name, typed neatly on the header alongside a charge of ADULTERY in big red letters.

His mirth echoed off the walls.

XIII

DEATH

Death

S ilently, he watched them feed.

The world had erred in classifying a gathering of ravens as an unkindness.

A plunder would be a better description. Though if one wanted to label a collection of beings with so heinous a mantle, *that* honor belonged to man.

Man's inability to display any kindness to his peers was legendary, even among the eternals.

Evidenced by the once lush, fertile field in front of him.

It reeked of death, strewn with victims of a hard fought battle. Bloated, decaying bodies from both armies, littered the countryside.

It mattered not whether it was man or beast; the dead invited the scavengers to feast.

The ravens swarmed en masse, pecking and fighting one another for the chance to tear morsels of desiccated flesh from drying bones. The frenzy persisted even after the birds could eat no more. They would feed until their bellies exploded.

All, except the largest of the ravens. He perched on a pile of skulls, observing in disgust.

He shook out his wings, as though cleansing himself of his repugnance for the gluttons surrounding him.

It was sad enough that man was so wasteful with the gift of life in order to lay claim to a nameless field, bearing witness to the aftermath was more than he could stomach.

Taking advantage of his disguise, Death soared upward to survey other portions of the bloody battlefield. As he flew, he became aware that something was amiss in this scene.

It was his responsibility to collect the souls of the recently departed, but there were none to be found. Every corpse was devoid of its mystical energy. A phenomenon Death had never encountered before, and it unnerved him.

Spotting a shape moving through the shattered remnants of a wooded thicket, he descended to one of the lower branches, talons digging into the splinters as he came to rest.

His head cocked to one side, he studied the shape's actions. Outrage propelled him from the branch when he recognized the insolence being perpetrated.

Boney feet planted firmly in the churned up, wet soil, Death emerged in his true form. His cloak and scythe, the indisputable trademarks of his existence, materialized at his command.

He was damned if — Death chuckled sardonically at his own wit because, he was indeed, damned — this interloper would see him naked.

The chuckle caught the shape's attention.

It paused.

Death seized the opportunity to address the figure.

"Might I ask what you are doing, friend? Those are *my* souls you are harvesting. I understand, given the magnitude of this carnage, you might have concluded… erroneously, I might add… I would not miss a few here or there. Rest assured, every soul here is accounted for," his tone, conversational.

"Is that so?" the figure responded indifferently, resuming its task. "Seems to me, you have been derelict in your duties."

Death stood, slack-jawed, at the creature's admonishment. Adding insult to injury, it had refused to show Death proper deference by facing him while delivering its reprimand.

The nerve!

Vexed, Death tapped the creature on the shoulder with his scythe. "Do you have any idea who you are addressing?"

The creature sighed at this second interruption. "As a matter of fact I do. You're a pompous, self-indulgent windbag, with nothing better to do than heckle me. Begone." It flicked a hand.

The creature returned to the small pile of bodies strewn haphazardly in the dirt, to collect the last of the souls the battleground had to offer.

Once full, the sack was cinched tightly around the neck, preventing any within from escaping. The interloper hoisted the burden onto its back and prepared to depart.

The field depressed the creature as much as it had Death.

The effrontery of this... this... stealer of souls, beggars belief, Death fulminated. *No respect.*

He saw red.

His scythe shredded the ancient material of the enchanted bag with ease, standing back as a deluge of souls erupted through the hole in the bottom, and vanished around the periphery of the battlefield.

The creature swung his gaze from the sack, now devoid of its load, to the toothy smile of Death.

Tossing it aside, the shadowy entity's hands came to rest on its hips.

Death readied himself for the backlash, which would

undoubtedly come in the form of a counterattack. His scythe gleamed brightly in the fading afternoon light.

He yearned for this confrontation but, in truth, could not have predicted what happened next.

The creature raised its arms to the shroud which concealed its features.

Instead of the mask of the dead, Death expected to see, his eyeless sockets widened with shock at the unparalleled example of feminine beauty in front of him.

The tall, slender woman contemplated him with shrewd dark eyes. Her long brunette tresses, captured by the teasing breeze, billowed around her. Her skin glowed with a brilliance even Death could not tolerate, forcing him to avert his gaze.

He knew her name from Japanese legends. *Izanami-no-Mikoto.*

Death was puzzled. Where was her brother, *Izanagi?* One never seemed to be without the other.

Unable to look at him, Izanami stared at the discarded bag, tapping her foot in exasperation.

"You are an unmitigated ass," she muttered balefully. "I was sent here by the gods to clear the field as a gift to you… despite having numerous responsibilities on my plate… all so you might be freed from your sentence of damnation.

"*But noooooo,*" Izanami huffed. "Your fragile ego was your undoing, yet again. Just as it was when you were human and took your own life, instead of tackling your fears and problems.

"Death — or should I say, Ernest? — no, because of your petulance, that is a name you shall never bear again," she scolded.

"I suggest you figure out how to mend the bag, because you'll be here a long time cleaning up your mess. Have an enjoyable eternity."

With that, she vanished.

Dumbfounded, Death remained motionless, blinking at the spot where she had stood. A crooked smile curved his face.

He never expected the Japanese goddess of death to be so exquisite. He had heard she resembled a withered old toad.

I guess you cannot believe everything written in myth and legend.

Nonchalantly, he spoke into the silence, "Do not forget to wish Izanagi well for me."

He gathered the bag and, with a shimmer of magic, sealed the hole. Grasping his scythe, he resumed the arduous task of clearing the field.

Resigned to serving his punishment for an eternity did not present an issue. In fact, suddenly, the air seemed fresher and the day not so bad.

The best part — he had job security!

About Rori Bleu

With a smattering of riverboat pirates and royalty in her heritage, Rori Bleu's childhood reflected her past. An interest in fairy tales, myth and legend were as important as spirited discussions around politics and current affairs — although some might argue they are one and the same!

A fascination, sparked by listening to Grimm's Fairy Tales at her grandmother's knee, not only encouraged Rori's passion for reading, but also steered her into the world of RPG's. What began as a fun pastime, soon evolved into the creation of fantastical worlds, but Rori never lost her love of politics going on to specialise in Governmental History and Historical Research.

Naturally this means her stories are steeped in historical accuracy and real-life intrigue. While Rori's love of a happily ever after means her preferred genre is romance, don't be surprised if you discover an occasional detour into historical fiction, thrillers, horror and fantasy.

To find more of Rori's books… click the link
https://linktr.ee/roribleu

About Rosie Chapel

Rosie Chapel lives in Perth, Australia with her hubby and two furkids. When not writing, she loves catching up with friends, burying herself in a book (or three), discovering the wonders of Western Australia, or — and the best — a quiet evening at home with her husband, enjoying a glass of wine and a movie.

Website: www.rosiechapel.com

Also by Rori Bleu

Pineapple Meringue

Imprisoned Hearts

Port of London

Dani's Masquerade

Black Tulips

Ajei's Destiny

Porta Aeternum

The Queen's Heart

Syn *with Matthew Forester*

Echoes and Illusions *with Rosie Chapel*

Evie's War *with Rosie Chapel*

Vindicta *with Rosie Chapel*

The Sela Helsdatter Saga *with Rosie Chapel*

A Flip of The Coin - Book One

Conceived Chaos - Book Two

Odin's Bane - Book Three

Also by Rosie Chapel

<u>Dystopian Romance</u>

Echoes & Illusions *with Rori Bleu*